I0615770

An Ordinary Story
of Extraordinary Hope

An Ordinary Story
of Extraordinary Hope

KEN R. ABELL

RESOURCE *Publications* · Eugene, Oregon

AN ORDINARY STORY OF EXTRAORDINARY HOPE

Copyright © 2010 Ken R. Abell. All rights reserved. Except for brief quotations in critical publications or reviews, no part of this book may be reproduced in any manner without prior written permission from the publisher. Write: Permissions, Wipf and Stock Publishers, 199 W. 8th Ave., Suite 3, Eugene, OR 97401.

Resource Publications
An Imprint of Wipf and Stock Publishers
199 W. 8th Ave., Suite 3
Eugene, OR 97401
www.wipfandstock.com

ISBN 13: 978-1-60899-656-8

Manufactured in the U.S.A.

All scripture quotations, unless otherwise indicated, are taken from the Holy Bible, New International Version®, NIV®. Copyright ©1973, 1978, 1984 by Biblica, Inc.™ Used by permission of Zondervan. All rights reserved worldwide.

Scripture taken from the HOLY BIBLE, NEW INTERNATIONAL VERSION®. Copyright © 1973, 1978, 1984 Biblica. Used by permission of Zondervan. All rights reserved.
The "NIV" and "New International Version" trademarks are registered in the United States Patent and Trademark Office by Biblica. Use of either trademark requires the permission of Biblica.

Scripture taken from the NEW AMERICAN STANDARD BIBLE®, Copyright © 1960, 1962,1963,1968,1971,1972,1973,1975,1977,1995 by The Lockman Foundation. Used by permission.

*For Anita Irene, whose steadfast love and patience
is beyond measure. She held my hand in all the dark places
and saw me through many desperate hours.*

&

*For our sons, whose forgiveness empowered me
to keep pressing on more often than they could ever know.*

&

*For our grandchildren, may their stories be overwhelmed
by extraordinary hope.*

&

*For those in these pages who are now
amongst the great cloud of witnesses.*

Grace

In a rant at God
  for long past pain
    a shadow of peace
      eclipses my brain.
My
  eyes
    collide
      with
a streaming sunburst of grace
that seems strangely
  out of place
on a gray-streaked landscape
  where whispers of defeat
    are grinning on a pale horse
      with no mercy, no remorse.
Grace
  marvelous
    amazing.
Mysterious
  wonderful
    grace
    still seems strangely
  out of place
where a wintry wind blows
  along a corridor of my soul
    and graveyard clouds
beckon me
  beckon me to surrender
    all my bright tomorrows
      to yesterday's deepest sorrows.
Yet each sunset
  brings a sunrise of hope
    where grace unfolds its petals
      like an old man stretching
        arthritic bones to wrap me
  in a fierce embrace that
    refuses surrender or defeat.

~KRA~

Contents

Author's Note

BIC is affectionate shorthand for the Brethren in Christ denomination. You can learn more about the best kept secret in North America by visiting www.bic-church.org

1

Prologue

"There is a time for everything, and a season for every activity under heaven: a time to weep and a time to laugh, a time to mourn and a time to dance . . ."

~Solomon~

THE PHONE RANG, SHATTERING the stillness of the June morning. It was too early for a phone call. I picked it up on the third ring. Tension immediately crept through me when I heard a canned mechanical-sounding voice say, "This is a collect call from the DeKalb County Jail from . . ." In the pause that followed my mind jumped as it filed through the names of men I had worked with in my ministry at the local jail in Whiteside County. A flash of irritation joined the tension as I wondered which one had now gotten in trouble with the law in DeKalb County.

The dead-air on the line was broken by a voice I knew well. It was strained and saturated with emotion, but it was definitely our third son.

"Wesley," he said in a barely audible whisper.

All the saliva instantly dried up in my mouth. I took the receiver away from my ear and looked at it, shaking my head in disbelief. I began listening again soon enough to follow the instructions to accept the charges and connect the call.

"Wesley?" I asked, confused.

"Yeah," he answered softly.

"What's going on?"

"I'm sorry, Dad," he said, choking out the words.

"What's going on?" I repeated, reaching for the arm of the chair to balance myself. All of a sudden I felt queasy, and my legs weren't working right.

"I guess I lost my head the other night."

"What's going on?" I asked again, sounding more than a bit stupid to my ears. I was seemingly unwilling or unable to grasp that this was our son Wesley on the other end of the line. And he was calling from jail. He had never given us a moment's worry all through his growing up years. He'd gone off to college three years earlier full of dreams to chase and a destiny to pursue, but now all those plans and high hopes were crashing and burning.

Anita came into the room, read my face, and asked, "What's wrong?"

I numbly shook my head and carefully lowered myself to sit on the edge of the chair. "Wesley," I whispered, "what's going on?" There it was again. I was like some idiot savant always coming back to the same question. I looked into Anita's eyes, and a wordless conversation passed between us. At some point I had stopped breathing, so I hitched in gulps of air, forcing myself to focus and listen.

The story gasped out in short, disjointed sentences. "I lost my head . . . I broke into an apartment . . . a fight happened. I stabbed the guy . . . nobody was supposed to be there. It's a class X felony. I didn't mean for it to happen . . . I stabbed the guy . . ." His voice was faraway and fading into hard sobs.

The words ice-picked at my brain. I sank into myself, clenched my teeth, and summoned up strength. In a moment of absolute clarity that came as a result of a lifetime's fascination with television crime shows, I asked, "Did you take the weapon with you or grab it in the apartment?"

"Took it with me," he replied, weak and shaky.

I swallowed, vaguely considering the legal implications. "What's going on in your life, Wesley?" I asked, much more sternly than intended. As horrible as the revelations had been so far, the answer that came across the wires startled me.

"Marijuana," he said flatly.

Silence. Lots of it racing back and forth between us. My gut instincts kicked in as I rapidly analyzed all the information he had shared. It didn't take much figuring to determine that something was missing; something just didn't add up.

Part of me wanted to scream and reach down the mouthpiece to shake him because it was obvious he was lying; lying to himself and lying to me. I wasn't a naive preacher fresh out of pastor's school and oblivious to the ways of the world. Little by little and bit by bit, innocence had been chipped away during my teen years, and since then I'd hit some holes and ditches, going to the bottom and back.

There had been times hanging out at after-hours backstreet dives when, if the law swooped in off the street for a round-up, I'd have been among those caught up in the sweep. I'd skirted along the edge of the drug culture with hardcore steelworkers, cabdrivers, and assorted other party animals, and those experiences told me that in this case, the truth was more complex than marijuana.

It may have been the first line he'd crossed on his descent into the madness that had him in jail, but simply using marijuana didn't explain the violent events he'd described. Smoking pot was surely a contributing catalyst, but streetwise seasoning said reality was likely buried beneath carefully constructed layers of self-denial and self-deception.

Over the next number of days and weeks, tears flowed freely as we worked at pealing back those layers to deconstruct his self-betrayal. Anita and I learned of a secret and desperate drug addiction that skewed his character and perspective. Marijuana was just the top of the recreational drug-use slide that spun downward in an out of control spiral of abuse and dependency.

The silence on the line thickened. A slow, steady sickness crawled through me. From some deep recess of memory, an anguished voice echoed, "O my son, Absalom! My son, my son Absalom! If only I had died instead of you—O Absalom, my son, my son!" King David's heart-wrenching lament at the news of his son's death had an eerie quality that gave me the creeps.

It was too real, too raw for me to immediately grasp. I shivered inside as the cadence of the words became a bitter rhythm building to some crazed crescendo. My head throbbed. The bitter rhythm increased its volume and hit its peak, and then in the pressured stillness which followed, a semblance of understanding squeezed me, pinching my mouth into a knowing smile.

The fact that a handful of ancient words from a long dead king of Israel spoke directly to my life didn't surprise me; there was no irony here. A cold comfort enveloped me. I wasn't alone. I glanced at Anita: We weren't alone.

Yes, there was great mystery in it, but somehow, in the midst of this unfolding tragedy, God was present with us. The One who had inspired King David to rise above the turmoil of his life was now walking with us to uphold us. I closed my eyes, nodded, and prayed. My body stiffened along with my resolve. In a heartbeat I went on automatic pilot. My emotions detached from my actions, and I sliced into the silence on the line.

"Wesley, I'll be over to see you today."

"Okay. I'm sorry, Dad." He was crying. And I realized that I was, too.

"Wesley?"

"Yeah?"

"I love you, son."

An affirmative response struggled out of him. And then we hung up.

In a blur, with our commitments for the day canceled or postponed, Anita and I were in the car. We spoke in hesitant tones as though we were picking at scabs to probe each other's wounds, and it hurt too much to do so. The empathy was easy and it strengthened us. It had been nurtured by an unknown number of wordless discussions over the years. Those moments of soft silence covered vast terrains, often bridging the distance between idealism and the reality of disappointments in a broken world.

There was no doubt that this latest manifestation of brokenness was going to require all the pulling together we could muster. We were approaching our twenty-ninth anniversary, and we were still standing because there were no secrets between us. Our relationship's steel backbone had been systematically strengthened in an experiential blast furnace where teardrops of joy and laughter were tempered by those shed because of heartaches and pain.

The road was a familiar stretch of northwestern Illinois. We'd lived there for six years. The landscape was an endless chain of corn and soybeans linked together by isolated farmhouses, occasional outcroppings of rural subdivisions and small towns.

Some humorist from the big city of Chicago, two hours to the east, might refer to the countryside as just the other side of nowhere, but the nation's heartland simply smiles at such remarks. It was completely comfortable with its role as a sprawling adhesive that held the diversity of the right and left coasts together.

Miles disappeared, along with an hour and a half. We found a parking spot outside the DeKalb County Jail in Sycamore, and then with a determined hesitancy, we exited the bright sunshine and made our way inside. It was disorienting. An officer behind sliding glass windows gave us directions.

Being a pastor meant that I could immediately get in to see him, but Anita would have to wait until the regularly scheduled visiting hours. We held hands for a terse moment, while the customary law enforcement activities transpired as though we weren't even present. Our hearts crushed, our minds overwhelmed and yet, life with its everyday normalcy kept chugging along all around us.

I released my grip, and then made my way through a heavy door and up the stairs to the second floor. Each step brought me closer to my son, but there was no joy or anticipation. The prickly feelings tied up within me were tightening into a tangled turmoil of knots. I consciously started monitoring my breathing. Slow, deep breaths; in through the nose, out the mouth.

It was then that I realized my teeth were firmly clenched and my jaw was hurting. I let out a long, low hiss of air and made a valiant but futile effort to relax as I buzzed the intercom. A disembodied voice responded, and we had a short dialog, then I sat and stared at the floor.

Within five minutes, a corrections officer came out to process me. She was obviously pregnant, which struck me as strange, but that thought quickly passed. Her authority was clear; she had a no-nonsense manner that demanded respect. She checked my identification, including my ministerial credentials, then had me empty my pockets and sign in.

Responding to her request, I assumed the position to be swept by the metal detector. It beeped on cue because of some titanium steel hardware in my left hip, which was a whole other story, but as it all unfolds, it'll get connected to this one. The guard warily accepted my explanation, then the door was opened and she ushered me through it.

When it closed, its electronic lock slid into place with a loud, sharp noise. The hard finality of the sound reverberated through me as I followed the officer along the wide corridor. It had been getting hot outside, but inside, the temperature was cool.

Perhaps the sterile atmosphere caused the coldness to be accentuated because an outbreak of goosebumps erupted on my arms. I half-walked half-shuffled into a narrow room that had four stools securely bolted to the floor and was told to wait for the prisoner to be brought out.

A few minutes passed, then Wesley and I were locked into the visiting area together. He was falling apart. His face was bloated and blotchy, his posture stooped and humbled. In the county-issue prison garb he looked curiously odd, like a disheveled scarecrow poking out of an oversized orange jumpsuit. His red-rimmed eyes were puffy and bloodshot; his unkempt hair jutted out at wild angles. A sense of desolation and aloneness cloaked him. Its force frightened me.

I hugged him, holding on tight as his body convulsed up and down in spasms of despair. It was painful to listen to the remorse pour out of him in jagged sobs. He was ashamed, and there was nothing he could do to change the past. He had made a whole slew of mistakes. Serious mistakes. He spoke of regrets. His guilt was self-evident, his contrition agonizingly real.

A volatile mix of sorrow and shame swirled within him, edging him to the precipice of hopelessness. His words inched terrifyingly close to suicide. We clung to each other, and as a tide of helplessness swelled within me, I silently listened.

He had never dreamed or planned to be a criminal; he hadn't given it much thought. That possibility had never been part of the equation. He'd been raised in a home of faith, though for much of his early childhood my tenuous grasp on it produced a love-hate relationship with God, which surely must have resulted in a mixed up confusion of messages.

What long-term effects did my thumbing my nose at God have on Wesley and his brothers? There remains some dark and lonely places where that question still tracks me down to tear me up inside.

Wesley was nine years old when I finally came to terms with God. I did my best to explain and make amends, but in matters of the heart and psyche, one never knows. Here, in the DeKalb County Jail, I was learning that, in his teen years, a carefully disguised rebellion against faith settled into him.

A series of increasingly poor decisions led him down an avenue filled with tragic detours. Now, confined to a cement block cubicle, fear nipped around the edges of every word he managed to choke out. He questioned the fairness of the system.

Some seasoned convicts had already filled his head with scams and unrealistic possibilities, but there was no escaping the facts. He'd done the crime, refused his Miranda rights, and confessed to it. He expressed a gut-wrenching mix of self-pity and sorrow.

After a fifteen-minute free-floating soliloquy, he arrived at the crux of the matter: Was there any hope? Was there any forgiveness for him?

The questions dangled between us as we ended our embrace. We sat on stools facing each other, our knees almost touching. A lump of emotion solidified in my windpipe as he soundlessly pleaded with me. Tears spilled down his cheeks. His chest heaved as he tried to steady his breathing. It was one of those forever moments that burns with every tick of the clock. After a long release of tension, his body slumped and his head bowed forward, his hair falling in a tangled mess.

I swallowed several times before my voice would function. I talked quietly, telling him about God's love and grace. He looked back at me with eyes that were vast pools of skepticism. In his severe anguish, hearing about an everlasting love seemed unreal and unreachable. He'd screwed up his life; he'd betrayed himself and his family; he'd hurt loved ones who cared about him; he'd ripped out his mother's heart and trampled on it. How could there be any forgiveness for him?

Undeterred by his despondent disbelief, I persisted in hushed tones, drawing empathy from the deepest well of my heart. Through the tears he nodded or slowly shook his head, alternating between wanting to hear hope and rejecting it.

I spoke for a long time about hope and redemption, easing the words out. A part of me was begging God to make the promise of those words real for both of us. We were interrupted when a guard rapped on the window, signaling that we had five minutes. I glanced at my watch to note we'd been together two hours.

Holding his hands, I prayed aloud, emptying myself of all pretenses as faith stitched together by desperation surged out of me in visceral phrases, sporadically punctuated by sobbing from both of us.

The corrections officer opened the door. We stood, and our arms vise-gripped around each other as he repeatedly whispered an apology that consisted of two overwrought words, "I'm sorry." They tattooed my eardrums as we unashamedly hung onto each other. It was tortuous. My heart was beating so hard that it actually hurt. I didn't want to let him go.

A gruffly muttered command from the jailer prompted us to finally release our hold. Our eyes connected for the briefest of moments, then in a flurry of motion my son was gone, and I had been escorted out. I surveyed my surroundings, kind of doing an internal reality check, then tentatively took the stairs down, my hand clutching the railing with each halting step.

∽ ∽ ∽

The remainder of that sorrow-filled day was swallowed by an unending silence. It was loud and scary as it echoed along canyons of memory where doubts and fears flourished beside flooded streams of bitter water poisoned by a whole slew of *what ifs* and *if onlys*. It was as though a great dam had shattered, unleashing a fierce flow of questions whose answers were relentlessly ambiguous.

Anita and I waded through it all together, but also alone. When the darkness of the day surrendered to the blackness of night, we went to bed, emotionally and physically exhausted. We prayed. Then, beside each other within this cocoon of unending silence, we tried to sleep. I stared at the ceiling for an indeterminate time, listening to her breathing.

When it slowed to the tell-tale pattern of slumber, I began reliving the day one more time, all the while asking God how we were going to stay strong through this. How was I going to be strong for Anita, for my family?

"O my son, Absalom! My son, my son Absalom! If only I had died instead of you—O Absalom, my son, my son!"

King David's plaintive exclamation came back as a thunderous stampede that rattled me and made me cover my mouth as though that would somehow prevent me from praying a similar prayer for my son, Wesley.

Wide awake, with seemingly every nerve ending frayed like bits of tattered twine, I rigidly fixed my eyes on the darkness, determined to stand strong. I'm not sure when or how it happened, but sometime in the consuming silence of the night, a peace settled on my mind, causing the turmoil to be still.

Enveloped by this calmness, the Spirit of the living God brought three principles to my attention; three principles that I'd preached in various venues because they were foundational to my faith journey and my understanding of Scripture.

As I half-prayed and half-meditated, a sweet trickle of hope warmed me from the inside out. I savored the precepts: *All of life is preparation, so everything happens for a reason; God works everything together for his purposes because his compassions never fail; to know and serve God is all that matters in life for in the grand scheme of eternity everything else comes to nothing.*

Invigorated by these truths, I began to remember God's faithfulness to me. In doing so I clearly heard my Grandma Major's wisdom, which was always delivered with a careful smile: "You think you got it bad? Take a look around. There's always someone worse off than you. Try counting your blessings."

Try counting your blessings. My lips creased. I hit the rewind button in my mind. Scenes began flickering in disjointed pieces. An old friend here, a schoolyard tousle there. None of them made sense, yet there was substance and a discovery that the past had prepared me for the present. As sleep came, I was far away from sadness, safe and secure within a memory of Scout Point.

2

Season of Pain

"Why, O LORD, do you stand far off?
Why do you hide yourself in times of trouble?"

~King David~

Scout Point was a little spit of rock beside Lakeshore Road. On the other side were the rusting remains of an old Boy Scout camp. I was six years old playing with my good friend. Her name was Queenie. She was a runt of a Bluetick Coonhound we'd rescued from a local dog pound.

We were inseparable from the moment I helped her out of the cage, which I seriously thought was jail. She was my first confidant, my first audience, listening attentively while I made up stories as we went along. There's no denying that she made a permanent connection to my heart.

It was a different time and a different place. There's no better way to describe my childhood than storybook. I grew up in Reebs Bay, a close-knit community nestled on the north shore of Lake Erie. The rhythms of life were as constant as the gentle summer waves swishing against the shale-stone bedrock of the shoreline.

Family, faith, and friends mingled together with chores, play, school, and church. Everyone knew everyone, and being neighborly was as natural as getting up in the morning to go to work. I learned about caring, compassion, and responsibility to others from the example lived by my parents and grandparents.

Life was adventurous. When I started school, Queenie and I began running with a semi-tough gang of friends. In time we came to be known as the Nice-guy Delinquents.

Mischief was our territory of choice. We looked for it everywhere. Nothing we did was vengeful or destructive, just harmless shenanigans in an era before political-correctness banned such exploits. On more than one occasion we managed to skirt along the edge of lawlessness without actually crossing the line.

We were would-be hoods, trying to figure out how to be Marlon Brando or James Dean in rural suburbia. The fact that we all came from reasonably stable two-parent homes kind of put a kink in our sense of rebellion, but we tried real hard.

In many ways life in Reebs Bay was idyllic. We frogged and fished every spring, skated and sledded every winter, and a hike to Sugarloaf Hill in any season had a pilgrimage quality to it. We played ice hockey in the winter, street hockey every other season, while fast-pitch softball filled our summers.

There was also the lure of Lake Erie. Wading through a sea of algae twenty-yards wide and two-feet deep to go for a swim in relatively clear water was a rite of passage carried out by only the bravest or stupidest among us. Given what we now know about pollution levels in the Great Lakes in the 1960s, it's astonishing that none of us ever came down with a rare disease or life-threatening infection.

At the Sunbeam Sunday School, which became the Port Colborne BIC Church shortly after I was born, faith in Jesus Christ was as genuine as it gets. It wasn't merely talked about; it was modeled, or at least that's the impression that has stayed with me.

It was there that I learned about Jesus, and it was a vaccination that took, getting into my bloodstream to become integral to who I am. When it happened, a song also embroidered itself on my psyche. It was springtime, and old-style revival meetings were being held. I was eight years old, sitting in a pew with my maternal grandparents, Percy and Geraldine Major.

The preceding summer, during a thunderstorm at a camp in northern Ontario, they'd slipped a truism into me that was about to be emphatically expanded. Much about that evening is lost, but what remains clear is what transpired in my heart.

The guest preacher was named Wilbur. In my eyes he was a big, red-faced man wearing a black suit and tie. He spoke with a poetic rhythm that immediately riveted my attention. The text and title of the sermon is long gone, but his booming voice painted word pictures about the greatness of God that had my imagination entirely engaged.

Each illustration was powerful, followed by the refrain: "My God, how great Thou art!" Layer by layer, he built the message about the magnitude of God's goodness, setting each point in the context of some natural wonder. I could see the places he described.

The final story had him standing on a mountaintop overlooking a bluegrass valley in Kentucky, and while shivers shot up my spine and my heart thumped mightily against my ribcage, he cried out, "My God, my God, how great Thou art!" Tears were streaming down his face. And mine.

While the congregation sang *How Great Thou Art* I responded to the invitation by going to the altar. Several others were kneeling there, and all the praying was accompanied by an ample amount of sobbing. I got on my knees, and an adult prayed with me. I was crying hard and feeling funny inside. Someone asked if I wanted to accept Jesus. I nodded, then was told to simply tell God I was sorry for my sins and ask Jesus to come into my heart, which I did with an intense sincerity.

There's absolutely no chance that a little boy's mind could understand the full ramifications of the words prayed. All I knew for sure was that I wanted to be forgiven and know this great God who loved me so much. And in looking back, the faith in Christ and strength of character nurtured in my upbringing steeled me for the years of turmoil that lay ahead. In hindsight it is easy to see that *all of life is preparation, so everything happens for a reason.*

The previous autumn, on or near my eighth birthday, my parents had taken me to the Port Colborne Library because I was finally eligible to borrow books in my own name. I was told that I was embarking on a great enterprise of never-ending knowledge, and nothing has ever deterred me from exploring the world around me in books of all shapes, sizes, and varieties.

The birthday present of a library card set off a life-long passion for a story well told and well lived. It also served to give me a refuge. No matter what the circumstances of my life, being in a room surrounded by books was always a place of comfort.

I would soon grasp the value of reading and appreciate the profound power of words and language. That awareness came about because of my first brush with sorrow, which involved my companion, Queenie.

It was December 1967, the beginning of a cold winter, when my old playmate got sick. I was twelve, and Queenie had been with me almost every day for seven years. We'd been to nowhere and back many times. We'd been everywhere and done everything together, learning our lessons along the way.

Queenie was a fertile bitch, giving birth to a litter of pups every spring I knew her, so she'd taught me something about life's wonders and mysteries. Then on the first day of January 1968, she up and died. Just the end consequence of living, but in my mind, the fleeting nature of friendship and the reality that life is temporary were hard facts to figure out.

My father and little brother carried buckets of hot water to a corner of our back yard to thaw the solidly frozen ground so they could dig a grave. I sat on the floor in my bedroom all by myself and cried. Every once in awhile, my mother or one of my older sisters would poke her head in to ask if I was okay or if she could do anything for me, but I wanted to be alone. It was a response to grief that I'd have opportunity to hone into an ingrained and sustained pattern.

In the introspection following my four-legged friend's death, I began to scribble my thoughts down, ascertaining quite quickly that I could work through or jettison ugly feelings by marking up good clean paper with my emotions.

The previous summer, when it was hot off the press, I'd read *The Outsiders* by S. E. Hinton. It captured my imagination in many ways, with its biggest impact being that it made me recognize I was a storyteller. And the stories I'd told Queenie or anyone else who'd listen could be written down.

My first real literary effort honored Queenie, a fine composition for seventh grade English class entitled, *Faith of a Bluetick*. It was well received, and since then, in one way or another, I've been writing or considering it.

Writing for no other reason than to write is often therapy. There have been some traumatic tangles that I've survived and ultimately escaped because of the cathartic aspect of writing. My creative awakening in the aftermath of bereavement has meant that I've never forgotten

Queenie. As the years passed, I've had other dogs, but none ever stole my heart like she did.

That is, until 2003, the September after Wesley was arrested when some people who loved me gave me a tiny hairball of a puppy, but that is a different part of the story. You'll have to keep turning these pages to determine if I connect all the pieces together.

In July 1969 Neal Armstrong walked on the moon. It made all the papers. The same month I had a freak accident in which I broke my left hip. It didn't make headlines anywhere, though the following spring I was featured in the *Port Colborne News*. A picture of me lying in a hospital bed was accompanied by an article, which in part read:

"Benched for baseball, but not for hockey. A fractured hip has Ken Abell out of baseball action this year but he is confident he will be goal tending again when hockey season rolls around."

My optimism about returning to the fray of ice hockey was pure fallacy because, even at the time, deep within me there was an awful comprehension that there'd be no promising athletic career for me.

I was in my fourteenth year when the fateful misfortune occurred. As I recall, it happened like this: Wainfleet Lions Club's Bantam-Midget All-star team was on the diamond, playing under the lights on the edge of Wainfleet Village. It was a perfect summer evening, with little swarms of bugs and mosquitoes gathering in moving pockets while stars began to twinkle in the dusky gray sky. The bleacher seats were speckled with spectators, but most of the fans were ringed around the ballyard in lawn chairs or sitting on the hoods of their cars parked behind the backstop. I was in the on-deck circle, taking it all in.

Our opponents were beating us bad, with their pitcher hurling smoke. I had what we referred to as a *toothpick* in my hands when I walked to the plate. It was a long, thin bat that had become my favorite. I recklessly eyeballed the pitcher, then surveyed the field. The bases were empty, and I was getting the signal to hit away. I stepped into the batter's box.

On the first pitch I shifted my weight, executing perfect mechanics as I swung at a hanging curve. The bat made solid contact with a loud crack that brought screams of delight from the hometown crowd. I don't know if I closed my eyes, got lucky, or employed some innate skill, but it was a frozen rope flare to the gap in right-center. I hustled out of the box and was down the line in a flash. The frantic first-base coach was windmilling his arms and hollering for me to round the bag and go to second base.

I made the turn, and now, as I remember it, everything was blurry slow motion because I don't know how what happened, happened. All I know for sure is that I slid into second base, which produced a cloud of dust and a burst of pain that scorched its way up my left side. I may have screamed; I may have writhed around on the ground; I may have cursed like there was no tomorrow. I'm sure my teeth were clenched and there were tears.

The umpire was bent over, his face inches from mine, asking if I was okay. And then the coach was kneeling beside me. He helped me up. It was excruciating. My left knee felt like it was in flames. Holding onto the coach, I tried to walk, but my left leg didn't want to work. I clutched both hands around it at the knee and forced it to take a step.

The whole leg had an electric tingle, generated by a ball of fire inside the knee. Others had gathered around me as I tentatively took a couple hobbling steps.

It hurt horribly, and there was queasiness in my stomach that had my attention. I thought I was going to throw up. Bile swirled up my throat, tasting sick and coppery as I swallowed hard to keep it down. There were shouts from the bleachers, but above the rumble of noise, I could hear my parents calling my name, with my mother's worry clearly carrying across the field.

"Walk it off, Kenny," my father hollered.

My parents were standing behind the backstop with my little brother and sister beside them. The mixture of love, pride and concern on their faces has stayed with me all my life. Or maybe just the sound of their voices created the picture in my mind so I could use it to motivate myself. All I can tell you for sure is that the photograph of them at that moment is prominently displayed in my gallery of memories. However, until I wrote this paragraph it had remained in the private collection.

Walk it off, Kenny. I closed my eyes, sucked in some air, grabbed guys on either side of me, and took a couple of steps. My mouth formed a sneer of a smile because it seemed as though I was going to be all right. The initial shotgun blast of pain had become this hot, burning sensation radiating from the knee. I was helped over to the bench, where they took my shoe and sock off, rolled up my pant leg, and examined my knee.

While they did so, the game resumed, with a pinch-runner standing on second base. Yeah, I had been safe, so that was something.

My father and little brother were close behind me. I'm positive that my mother wanted to be there, too, but in her code of honor, there was no chance she'd ever embarrass me by nurse-maiding me in front of my teammates. She stayed by the backstop with my baby sister.

Dad, the only coach I ever had, was crouched behind me, his big fighter's hands on my shoulders. He had a conversation with the other adults checking out my knee, and the consensus was that I'd be fine in a few weeks because the injury was *just* torn ligaments.

That provided some solace then, though the diagnosis would turn out to be much more complicated. I stared blindly at the field, not having any inkling that the consequences of that split-second bit of aggression, stretching a single into a double, would color my perspective for the rest of my natural life.

In March 1970, after many frustrations because of repeated misdiagnoses, I was admitted to what was then known as the Welland County General Hospital. The previous eight months had become a walking nightmare, or more precisely from my viewpoint, a limping nightmare. Pain and I had become inextricably linked as I developed an awkward, lopsided gait that inspired extremely cruel nicknames, some of which can still make me cringe inside.

The immediate aftermath of the ballpark incident found me on crutches, with my left knee iced down and wrapped up on a daily basis for several weeks. Our family doctor concluded that it was indeed torn ligaments, prescribing the crutches and course of treatment. During the initial examination, no X-rays were taken. Much later, when the pain persisted, he ordered X-rays, but only of the left knee, which revealed nothing. One time when I was leaving the office after my third or fourth visit as a result of my damaged leg, I heard the word *psychosomatic* used by a nurse, and directed at me.

That was a new one for my vocabulary, so I looked it up in the dictionary. What I read infuriated me at first, but it crept into my consciousness, then as the months dragged by with no progress or improvement, I started to grimly wonder about my attachment to sanity.

My parents were zealous in their efforts to find out what was going on with my leg. They traveled all over southern Ontario to take me to a dozen or more clinics and doctors, some of which, we decided were just slightly above snake oil salesmen. I hated being the focal point of all this attention and dealt with it by withdrawing more and more.

In hindsight, with the benefit of much reading and several discussions with orthopedic surgeons, here's what actually happened. I likely had a congenital defect in both hips, which would have corrected if puberty had been allowed to continue with no shock or trauma to the joints.

Since I had never presented any symptoms, there was no reason to suspect there was danger in me playing sports. The slide into second base at that critical moment and angle merely exploited the weakness with which I'd been born. It was no one's fault; it was simply life and life only. The ball of my left femur sheared off clean, and with remarkable deftness, lodged itself into soft tissue. The femoral neck slipped back into the socket.

The prescribed protracted time on crutches, keeping weight off the left leg, allowed the hip joint to adjust to its new configuration. Through all of this, there was never any pain in the hip itself, but the knee was an ongoing agony.

Room 303-S of Welland County General Hospital became home. In the midst of adolescence, I spent six months there, with four of those flat on my back, much of those in a full body cast. I underwent three major operations, with the first one lasting an epic six and a half hours.

After the work was completed, the surgeon emerged to explain things to my parents. He told them that the damage had been extensive, and despite his best efforts, it was iffy that he'd been successful. The growth plate had been severely wounded, coupled with the fact that the blood supply to the femoral head had been disrupted for such a long period, meant that it could be devastating. Only time would tell if healing and regeneration would occur. If not, he'd have to amputate my left leg.

That nasty piece of information was withheld from me for several years, which was likely a good thing. When I heard it, I felt sorry my parents shouldered that knowledge by themselves, but it swelled within me a tremendous admiration for their enduring grit and grace.

The snapshot and article in the *Port Colborne News* came a few short days after that first operation, when the ultimate outcome of the surgery was in grave doubt. No one would've ever figured that from the brave front put forward by my parents. I never heard any discouraging word or suggestion that there would ever be anything except a thorough recovery.

They may have had deep moments of private anguish, but the rest of the world saw only confidence. From what reservoir did they draw their strength and hope?

The answer was obvious. Though my father was not a church-going man he had an abiding faith in God rooted in the elemental truth of Micah 6:8: *To do justice, to love mercy and to walk humbly with God* was the creed by which he aspired to live. My mother had carried me to church as an infant, read Bible stories to me, and spoke openly of her belief in a God who allowed no accidents or coincidences. Everything that happened had a reason.

With such an example set, there was no time or place for tears. My parents had tempered me with mental toughness. Their combined force of will gave me the courage to overcome this setback. I steadily bore down into myself.

In that process, I discerned a complex curiosity about the connection between words and feelings that demanded exploratory probing. I discovered Edgar Allan Poe, and as covertly as possible, began to read more and more poetry from the realm of pain and loss. It didn't sadden nor depress me, but rather, its common ground fortified me.

Little did I know that around a bend in the fast-approaching future, a series of events would transpire that'd make a fractured hip seem like a remote occurrence, or that I would be tapping all the emotional resources available to me just to stay balanced and keep putting one foot in front of the other.

In November I was given the go-ahead to begin putting weight on the left leg. No more feather-steps with the crutches. The green light came after several months of sporadic therapy that emphasized the necessity for me to always be careful. I was told to pamper the hip and always make allowances for it. There was a long list of restrictions drilled into me, all the things I could never consider doing or trying.

By today's standards that would be regarded as the wrong approach, but it was what their understanding was at the time. I was something of a sponge, a sensitive and impressionable young man, soaking up everything I heard. The counsel to baby the hip got inside my head, causing a self-image to gradually evolve that was hurtful and perhaps more destructive than the physical injury. In my mind, I was a carnival freak securely sequestered on the sidelines of life. That twisted self-portrait would keep me in second-guessing mode for a long time.

There were quirky aspects to learning how to walk all over again as a teen-ager. It was weird and a little scary at the beginning because doubt and failure had filled my head. The first momentous step was a family event, complete with cheers, laughter, and tears.

It was a regular weekday evening. We'd had supper together, then Mom announced that she'd received an important phone call that afternoon. She kept the suspense alive for awhile as we peppered her with questions, then simply said that the doctor had called to inform us that it was time for me to start walking.

We all went into the living room. I used the crutches to get there, which set off hoots of raucous laughter from my brother. Apparently he figured I was supposed to automatically walk without them, which certainly would have been nice. As it turned out, it wouldn't be that easy. The fear of falling or that the leg had lost its usefulness had gotten ingrained in me.

Mom stood behind me in the hallway while my father positioned himself across the room in front of the door. My siblings gathered on the couch as my personal cheerleaders. I tried numerous times to simply let go of the crutches, but even with all the encouraging words of affirmation, they remained glued to my side, with my hands clenched around the grips. My apprehension mutated into a tension that thickened the air.

Anxiety clogged my throat. "I can't do this."

"What do you mean, *you can't do this?*" Dad asked. He had a smile on his face and a twinkle glinting in his eyes, but there was a stern inflection in his voice that whiplashed my attention. There was no point in me saying it again; there was no point in trying to explain what I meant or what was going on inside my head.

I straightened myself and drew a deep breath, then, without any warning, I dropped the crutches and pressed forward. Leading with my left leg, which didn't tingle nor collapse out from under me, I took two steps before getting lifted off my feet in a gigantic bear hug.

Dad was bellowing laughter as his powerful arms crushed me. He'd been a boxer and wrestler before I ever knew him, a physically imposing man with a volatility and affability which were both legendary. His capacity for anger was equaled only by his all-encompassing sense of humor, with both expressed in roars. When he put me back on the floor, I noted that Mom was crying happy tears.

What do you mean, you can't do this? For an hour or so everyone took turns walking me around the house, holding my arm as though *their* stability depended on it. Even my four-year old sister took a giggling try at it, which had us all laughing. My strides were short and tentative, with many pauses, but my left leg was doing its job. It was a half-inch shorter than the right one, but it was doing its job.

It quickly became apparent that there was a distinctive hitch in my step. In the years ahead, depending on my mood, it'd be viewed as an ugly souvenir or a badge of honor.

In February 1971 my father was nursing a toothache. Early on the morning of the fifteenth, as he stooped over to tie his work boots, I asked how it felt. He replied that it wasn't bothering him too much, but that he knew it would begin hurting once he got outside in the cold. They were the last words I'd hear him say. He went out the door, never to return home again.

At around 2:20 that afternoon, at Port Colborne Quarries, his throbbing jaw didn't matter anymore. Nothing mattered anymore because he was killed in an industrial accident. He didn't fall asleep; he didn't shuffle off the mortal coil; he didn't pass away; he didn't simply die; he didn't get transferred to glory, or any of those other soft-soap euphemisms. He was *killed*. A month earlier, he'd celebrated his forty-second birthday, and until that horrid day when his body was crushed by a fully-loaded Euclid dump truck, he'd been as healthy as the proverbial horse.

My father's death was a seismic event in our family. If a Richter-scale existed that could measure earthquakes on the emotional and spiritual landscape, then on February 15, 1971 it would've peaked completely off the chart into some unknown cataclysmic territory. Even after all these years, the after-shocks continue to ripple in our lives.

In March 2008, after a valiant struggle with a vicious infection, my mother died. A few weeks before she drew her last labored breath, God gave me a precious gift which I treasure. I got to sit beside Mom's bedside and visit. Just us. She was lucid and clear-minded, and of all things, she wanted to talk about *that* day. She replayed it hour by hour, sometimes recalling minute details.

From time to time, I prompted her with a question about this or that, but mostly I listened. It was explicitly clear to me, not for the first or likely the last time that what's sketched on the blackboard of our souls in trauma never gets erased.

My brother and sisters each have their intense experiences of *that* day and the difficult days that followed. I could tell them here because we have shared them repeatedly, but memories, especially disquieting ones, are extremely personal, so I'll endeavor to not cross any lines. Though, being entirely forthright, there may be blending that can't be helped because our stories and lives are intertwined.

I was fifteen years old. I had been walking without a cane for less than a month, with the trademark limp getting permanently programmed into my brain. When we got off the school bus at the end of Woodlawn Drive, my older sister, Janice, ran on ahead of me. The sun was shining low in the west, with the sky beginning to be embraced by long gray fingers of twilight.

It was cold and getting colder. I matched a cigarette I'd bummed from someone on the bus, acting like a wannabe tough guy, smoking it down to the filter before ditching it. A clandestine flirtation with nicotine was swiftly developing into addiction.

When I came around the slight bend in the road at Murphy's Lane, I stopped. Something was going on; something was wrong. Our house was less than a hundred yards farther. There were a half-dozen or more cars parked in and around our driveway. I recognized some, but not all of them. My mind took off, imagining some dreadful incident involving my mother or little sister. I had the presence to pop a couple mints into my mouth, then hurried up and shuffled into a hop-step spurt because I wasn't allowed to actually run like a normal person.

Grandpa Major and Uncle James came out of the front door when I arrived at our sidewalk. Their manner was subdued as they walked directly to me, their eyes alternating between looking at me and flitting away. It was evident that they had both been crying, which made no sense whatsoever.

"I got some bad news, Kenny," Grandpa said softly. He placed his hands on my shoulders as my uncle slipped in behind me.

"What happened to Mom?" I asked, sounding angry.

"Nothing. It's your Dad. He was killed at work today." There were these huge tears in my grandfather's eyes, spilling down his weathered cheeks.

I knew he was giving it to me straight, but something inside me unglued itself and started flapping around in an uncontrolled frenzy.

"No, Grandpa. No. You're lying." With the distance of miles and years, I still marvel that I verbalized that accusation because it's impossible to envisage a circumstance that would've ever caused my grandfather to utter an untruth. He was a profoundly honorable man who taught me many lessons about character and perseverance that remain a part of me to this day. But I called him a liar, not once but twice. It whispered out of me, "*You're lying, Grandpa.*"

"No, he's not, Kenny. Your father's dead," my uncle said flatly.

"Kenny." Grandpa gave me a little shake. I looked into his eyes. "You have to be strong for your mother. You're the man in the family now," he said, nodding in a slow steady manner. "Do you understand?"

Do you understand? All of a sudden, that thing that had come loose inside me stopped cold, stiffened, and locked itself down. The happenings of our interior lives are mysterious. In an instant, acquiescence to this new reality sank its roots deep into me. I had two older sisters, a younger brother, and a baby sister. I was in the middle, and the oldest male, which, because of the way I had been raised, meant that I had no choice. My father had taught me to be the man of the house. Now that he was gone, here was my grandfather reminding me of my obligation, and soon several uncles would be reinforcing those same instructions.

There was nothing mean-spirited or improper in their admonitions. Indeed, it was the only kind of things that could be offered by hardworking men wise to the sometime random harshness of the world, but in my mind, the expectations were overwhelming. No one, especially me, had any perception what my heightened sensitivity would do with those words or how badly they'd mess me up. There were no bereavement or crisis counselors available to walk any of us through the shock or help us process feelings. I don't know if they even existed back then. If they did, we certainly never knew anything about them in Reebs Bay.

My grandfather's hands were heavy on my shoulders. We stared at each other soundlessly, with little white wisps of our breath puffing between us. I gave a tiny nod. He responded likewise. In that wordless conversation, a great transaction occurred.

On *that* day, before a single tear for my father watered my eyes, a passage took place. Grief, along with all the remnants of childhood, was appropriated by the demands of adulthood. I accepted the mantle of responsibility without reservation or hesitation.

In the sports terminology that had been so much a part of my upbringing, I sucked up my despair to do what needed to be done for the family. I would rapidly find myself thrust into situations beyond my realm of ability or knowledge. I was neither prepared nor emotionally equipped to be a man, and likely failed miserably at it, but I did the best I could.

We went into the house together. The living room was packed with people. My mother was on the couch, her face blotchy, her eyes raw, her hands in her lap twisting a handkerchief. I sat beside her, took her hands, and listened as she told me that Dad wouldn't be coming home tonight.

It was a surreal scene. All these friends and relatives milling around speaking in hushed tones while shooting furtive glances at my mother as she spoke with a detached certainty that startled me. I muttered some useless phrases, then we looked directly into each other's eyes for an extended period of time.

The murmur of voices in the room went far away. Her eyes were pools of pain, but swimming there was this steely determination. I don't know if I gave Mom anything on *that* day, but the firm resolve glinting in her eyes was a comfort and encouragement to me.

The moment passed. Someone entered the living room and said something that took my mother's attention. It was my opportunity to disengage. I did so and wandered out to the kitchen where I had some meaningless and hopefully forgotten conversations with my siblings. I put it that way because we were all numb and reeling, emotionally unraveling. Our feelings were peeled back and frayed. We said pointless things as we struggled to make sense of this tragedy too close and too ghastly to be real. I do recall a single sentence spoken by me to my little sister, Jennifer, which prayerfully fell by the wayside because in the annals of history they're among the stupidest words to ever stain the air.

At some point, before it got too dark, I slipped out of the house to walk over to the beach. Dusk was settling on the darkest day of my life. I sat on the bench, glad to be alone. The lake was a frozen wasteland, with the shoreline piled high with uneven mounds of ice created by the ever-shifting currents. Not too many days earlier my brother, Rob, and I had been climbing around on them and having fun pretending we were exploring some unmapped mountain range. I vaguely wondered if we'd ever have fun again.

Night fell from the sky, creating shadowy recesses for my eyes to probe as I prayed like I'd never prayed before.

It was one word: "*Why?*"

It came out as a choked whimper, then I asked again a bit louder. I waited and waited. And waited some more. When no answer came, tension coiled up within me like a cobra preparing to strike. I clenched my teeth and screamed the question at the top of my lungs. It shattered the stillness, hanging in the gloom for a moment before echoing back to taunt me.

That echo was destined to stay with me for more years than I can number. It came back again and again. There were to be many more tragic accidents which would cause the question to reverberate to my core. I searched for the answer in lonely isolation. It became the platform on which I stood to shake my fist at God, until one day when I was deep in the belly of a beast that was consuming me I came across God's answer to Job.

One phrase snapped off the page and hit me so hard I may have winced. In the *New American Standard* which I was reading at the time, it says, "Now gird up your loins like a man. . ." I immediately interpreted it to mean: *Stand up and be a man.*

That revelation would be in the future. When it found me, it rocked me back on my heels because of how I'd shed the taunting echo on *that* day. I silenced it by tenaciously deciding to stand up and be a man. I didn't know what it meant or what all would be involved, but when I left the beach to walk home, it was in my mind that I wasn't going to disappoint my grandfather or dishonor my father.

When I got back, the house was even more crowded than earlier. I'm sure all the visitors were friends, neighbors, or relatives, but seriously, there could have been a few off the street and no one would have ever noticed. There were people coming out of the woodwork. I don't know if I had been missed or not, but I doubt it because there was so much activity. Everyone had brought food, so there were casseroles and covered dishes on the table, stove-top, and counter.

My oldest sister, Jane Ann, who in a time of innocence was known as Sissy, fixed me a plate and told me I had to eat all of it. She was a married woman now. Her wedding had been the previous June when I'd been in the hospital. It'd been planned long before my unfortunate confinement, and it couldn't be changed. The wedding party and assorted relatives swung by my room to include me in some pictures, which turned out to be rather rewarding for me. Uncle Frank was the last to leave, and when we were alone he gave me a vigorous handshake, sliding me a couple twenty dollar bills in the process, and told me keep it to myself.

Late *that* night, Uncle Frank, who was married to my father's sister, sat at our kitchen table chain smoking and drinking black coffee. He was a general contractor, an old-school man who approached every task, no matter how mundane or routine, as though it was vitally important and worthy of his best efforts. His hands were always busy, and he could do some amazing things with bits of wire and electrical tape. He was perhaps the original jack of all trades.

Dad had driven a dump truck for him and with him, and lots of times I'd tagged along on the jobs. There was a greasy-spoon truck stop we'd hang out in for meals or breaks in the day. It had a pinball machine, and I don't know how he did it, but whenever I played, Uncle Frank rigged it so my nickel would last game after game after game.

Port Colborne was a small blue-collar town. Secrets, when they existed, didn't remain hidden for long. Everyone seemed to have some connection to everyone else. Gathering information was merely a matter of knowing who to ask, and because of Uncle Frank's association with Port Colborne Quarries through his business, it was from him we learned some inside details about the accident. I can't say with any certainty who else was in the room when he held court, but it was crowded.

I sat in a corner of the kitchen, on a chair beneath the phone on the wall, and listened to every word, hurting in ways beyond description. I heard savage stuff that still has the capacity to wake me up in the middle of the night. Uncle Frank had these big expressive eyes which always seemed to be gleaming toward laughter, but not *that* night. They were flinty hard and edgy, filled with an unmistakable disbelief.

He spoke straight-forwardly, with each new fact punctuated by a long pull on a cigarette or a swig of coffee. He had an attentive audience, with everyone hushed. Little did any of us know that in less than a year, Uncle Frank would be dead, the victim of his own violent accident.

In January 1972, Uncle Frank was buried alive when the foundation he was digging collapsed on top of him. It happened in Wainfleet Township, not far from his shop alongside the highway. My sister, Janice, was the one who told me. I'd stayed late at school for reasons long since forgotten, and she was there to meet me when I got off the bus. It was already dark, and I was surprised she was in the car waiting for me. I had expected to walk home and was actually looking forward to it.

"What's up?" I asked, climbing into the passenger seat.

She was crying. "Uncle Frank was killed."

In the eleven months since *that* terrible day, Janice and I had spent many late nights and early mornings sitting in our kitchen trying to be strong and supportive. We'd clawed our way through emotional wreckage, often in complete silence as we munched on midnight meals of fish sticks. Now her words were unreal, shimmering in the space between us like little shards of glass that'd cut us if we examined them too closely. We rode home without saying anything else because sometimes words are worthless absurdities that only serve as complications.

Uncle Frank was killed. The horror of it, coming so soon after the brutality of my father's death, was too much to absorb. I wanted to run away and hide. In many ways, in the days immediately following, I accomplished that goal. I sat in the exact room at the same funeral home that'd housed my father's coffin, staring at another closed casket, but my mind had checked out. All the hopelessly helpless banalities of well-meaning friends stayed with me only long enough for me to note that I'd heard it all before.

My one-word prayer was frequently voiced, "Why?"

No answer was forthcoming, so I disappeared inside myself to nurture an ugly bitterness. I was sixteen years old, and a sense of impending doom was creeping into my thought patterns. After the funeral, I did what I was quickly becoming expert at doing; I swallowed hard, denied my feelings, and moved on.

Later that year, I had another opportunity to hone my denial skills when a boyhood running buddy was killed in an automobile accident. His pickup truck had gone off the road, rolled over, and hit a culvert. The morning after, I heard about it at seven o'clock on CHOW Radio.

Several of us went to the compound where the vehicle had been towed. It wasn't completely demolished, and that surprised me. It was dented up some, and the windshield was one huge spider-web crack, but it didn't appear bad enough for someone to have died. Maybe the radio report had it wrong, but then I looked inside. The dashboard and roof were splattered with blood; my friend's blood.

His name was Peter, and as quick as quick can be, he was dead. We'd played marathon street hockey tournaments in front of his house. I'd seen him a week earlier at the Wainfleet Fall Fair, and we'd had a good talk, and now he was gone. I remember him often because, without a doubt, he was the funniest person I've ever known. He had a joke or one-liner for every occasion and a laugh that remains embroidered in memory.

It was autumn 1972. I had just turned seventeen. It seemed that violent death was stalking me. I didn't consciously dwell on it, but it was always there in the background, catching my attention from time to time. Mostly I choked off the questions and emotions churning inside me, smothering them little by little and bit by bit.

I couldn't show weakness because my mother, younger brother, and sister needed me. I wasn't equipped to attend parent-teacher events at school, but I played that role as best I could, along with other similar assignments that summoned a maturity in me that I neither felt nor particularly desired.

I sought solace in my faith. I drew close to God and rapidly discovered that he kept his word. He drew close to me. I dug through the Bible with a passionate intensity, searching for meaning and purpose. When I look at the KJV edition I used at the time, I can hardly fathom the scope of my notes and jottings. I explored complex issues usually reserved for professors and scholars.

While in this season of study, surrounded by a knot of committed believers, I came to know that God was calling me into the ministry. It took many long months of praying alone and with dedicated friends who cared for me at the deepest possible level. The experience of those relationships still impacts me even after all these years. The final confirmation happened on New Year's Eve and was so clear it gave me goosebumps. I knew what I knew; there could be no denying the enormity of it.

At first I was thrilled, and so were those who had journeyed in prayer with me. Some of the wisest and most instinctive counselors I've ever had came alongside to help me plan my life accordingly. There were

Bible Colleges to check out, but also some things I could do that'd be good preparation.

Our youth group started going around to different churches doing a music presentation, and I'd give my testimony or even preach a feeble sermon. We were always well-received, and I kept hearing more and more affirmations of God's call.

Unknown to anyone, something bad was going on inside me. There was a slow-working poison of untapped grief festering. I had the outward appearance of strength and stability, but inside I was a teetering wall ready to crash down.

The toxin of unresolved grief had given me an old man's heart and a whipped puppy's need to cower in some dark corner. I didn't know what to with all the sick feelings. To me it was entirely natural to suck it up and keep pressing on.

That winter, a program called Summer Service blipped on my radar screen. It immediately excited me. Much more than that, it became an obsession; I *had* to go. My mother, siblings, and grandparents were extremely supportive. The whole call to pastoral ministry was slightly weird in some branches of the extended family, but mostly I received encouragement. I took charge of the short-term mission trip idea. I'd have to do a juggling act with other responsibilities, but it was an opportunity not to be missed, so after considerable prayer and discussion, I applied.

Zane Grey had lit up an adventurous attraction to the old west in me, so my first choice was Navajo Mission. A distant second was Camp Brookhaven, a ministry of Fellowship Chapel in the Bronx, NY. I was a longtime Yankees fan and had recently read *The Cross and the Switchblade* by David Wilkerson with great interest, but even so, when I received news of my appointment to Camp Brookhaven, I was deeply disappointed. Though I've tried to work the logistics several times, as I write this, I still haven't been to Navajo Mission.

However, apparently God has a plan, and he knows what is best for us. The One who spoke the universe into existence has intricacies far beyond the realm of our finite comprehension. Even after examining how God's sovereignty has played itself out in my life, I'm not sure why I often still struggle with it. What I learned and who I met in New York City would change my life. And by way of foreshadowing, it'd give some insights into how God was working tragedy together for his purposes.

≈ ≈ ≈

It was summer 1973. Richard Nixon was doing a political high-wire act that ultimately became a free-fall and will forevermore be known to history as Watergate. It was an exciting and complex time, and I was enthralled by it all. *What did the President know, and when did he know it?* Packing my bags in late June, I wondered how I was going to stay plugged into the news on the road.

Before flying to New York City out of Harrisburg, PA there was a gathering of the BIC clan at Messiah College for the General Conference Quiz Finals. I was there as a member of the Port Colborne BIC Church Quiz Team. We were tight. A tightness that remains even though we only see each other every twenty years or so, but at that meet, Canadian Conference Champions or not, we were completely swamped by the competition. We folded the tent quickly, but in the relational and knowledge development department we were definitely winners.

My teammates saw me off at the Harrisburg Airport, where I bought a newspaper and read it cover to cover on the flight to LaGuardia Airport. It was the first day of July. The Senate Watergate Committee was still holding their televised hearings, so the possibility of daily revelations was ever-present.

If someone would have told me on the plane that, by bedtime, Nixon's troubles and intrigues would be relegated to the nether regions of my concerns, I would have laughed aloud, but if someone had made that observation, he or she would have been exactly right.

It happened in a heartbeat, but first there was a harrowing trip to the Bronx, with a future missionary at the wheel and another in the passenger seat. Both were seemingly unaware of my near panic in the back seat as the car weaved crazily in and out of heavy traffic. We whizzed by burnt out cars and dilapidated buildings.

My eyes were likely saucers as I tried to incorporate everything I was seeing into the matrix of my perspective. There were provocatively clad ladies on several street corners, and more than one instance of children playing in water spewing out of fire hydrants, which, I was to learn, were referred to as *johnny-pumps*.

After arriving safely, I ambled over and bought a slice of pizza at a hole in the wall joint on Tremont Avenue, then sat on the steps of Fellowship Chapel to eat. This was a whole different reality, and I was just beginning to grasp the fact that I was a long way from home. That was confirmed when a guy came bopping up the sidewalk. In an open and friendly manner I asked, "How you doing?"

"What you looking at, man!" was his twitchy-eyed reply. His head swiveled as he went past, keeping suspicious eyes on me until he was a half-block away.

Welcome to New York. Indeed, I wasn't in Reebs Bay anymore.

It was late in the day when I was transported to Camp Brookhaven, eighty or so miles north of the city. The campus was set on a small hillside on both sides of a fairly busy road. The buildings were white with dark green trim.

After stowing my gear in a cabin, I was directed to where the staff was gathering. I walked up the grassy slope and entered a screened-in porch abuzz with conversations. A group of twenty or so was sitting around tables eating.

As it turned out, I was the last to arrive. I filled an open spot at one end of the room, slapped some mustard on a boiled hot dog, then took a bite to learn that the bread was slightly frozen. It was cruddy in my mouth, but I munched away and surveyed the room. Like an unknown number of loner heroes in western novels, I was consciously measuring each person, weighing who they were and where they came from, but then that intentionality took a nosedive into oblivion.

Across the room sat this strawberry-blonde who was following my gaze. When it landed on her, our eyes held for a brief second as she smiled directly at me, and with that fleeting sparkly-eyed flash, it was lights out for my heart. All of a sudden, a lousy hot dog on a slice of icy bread was exceptional cuisine, thank you very much. I felt flush. I wondered if anyone else noticed; I wondered *what* had just happened. I didn't know where to put my eyes. She was wearing a pretty yellow blouse with a strategically placed display of butterflies and flowers, but even a rube from the wilds of Wainfleet knew he couldn't linger on that spot for long.

In the interest of full disclosure, I must tell you that I was as normal as the next seventeen-year-old-male. There was nothing wrong with my hormones; they were alive and kicking. I had briefly dated a couple girls and instinctively flirted with anyone who looked my way, but I didn't want a girlfriend. I knew many girls who were good friends, but wasn't in the market for a serious relationship. I had another year of high school, then four or five years of college.

None of that mattered much after that instantaneous connection across the room. My brain was sending an urgent alarm to my heart, but the warning was garbled in transmission, so was inevitably unheeded. It was too late because my heart was untethered and racing over the cliff. I did my best to steal sneaky glances at this nameless beauty who seemed to be employing a similar stealth to check me out.

We went around the table introducing ourselves. Since I was the latecomer, it was decided that I'd be the first to share. I have no idea what I said, but I'm sure, given the hitch in my breathing and rising blood pressure that I demonstrated what the phrase tongue-tied truly meant. Each took their turn, though I don't recollect a single detail. When my eyes weren't darting in her direction, I was looking outside, watching fireflies as I tracked a countdown until we'd get to the sparkly-eyed girl.

Finally it was her turn. My attention was riveted. She looked straight at me, gave another of those flashing smiles, and said, "My name is Anita."

I was gone. I was out beneath the stars doing cartwheels across the dewy grass and vicariously flitting around with the fireflies. Nothing else she said in that moment has remained. I was captivated by the appealing promise of her eyes, so the rest of the evening happened in a fog. We were given basic orientation, with others asking questions and getting some answers. Then we played a few getting acquainted games.

Through all the interaction, Anita went out of her way on more than one occasion to poke fun at the distinctive *out* and *about* aspects of my Canadian accent. She acted like she had known me forever, and that easy demeanor broke down barriers inside me. She possessed a spontaneous empathy that unnerved me in a good way. In the next few days, she'd pry open a creaking dungeon in my soul and excavate feelings I didn't even know I felt.

It was somewhat funny that, in the beginning, we related to each other under false presumptions. I thought she was sixteen, while she thought I was twenty-one. Upon discovering our true ages, we laughed so hard we cried. Born and raised in the mountains of Pennsylvania, she was twenty and a college student, and I was a seventeen-year-old high schooler with a bunch of big ideas and that's about all. The age difference was of no consequence to us. There was no turning back. We were in love.

Emotions are tricky things. The heart has a will of its own that can be complex and mysterious. Hypothetically speaking, there are many doubts about whether or not people can actually fall in love at first sight. I don't know about others, but for me, after closely examining experiential evidence, I flat-out guarantee that for us that's what happened. That night, when our eyes made contact across the tables, while I absently chewed on a bite of hot dog, love happened.

The first bus load from the Bronx arrived the next day, and we were thrust into camp life, dealing with the different worldview of inner-city children. With our days filled with counselor responsibilities, we manufactured ways to be together. Early every morning there were long walks as we took roundabout routes to staff devotions. Remarkably, our separate teams were always paired up for group activities, and while hanging out on the fringe, we'd quietly converse.

We also managed to be on the same preparation or clean-up crew for many of the meals. During some down time late one afternoon, we sat off by ourselves in a corner of the dining hall, and while playing Dutch Blitz, we shared our stories. The game quickly became redundant, but we kept shuffling and reshuffling the cards, apparently thinking it'd be best to keep up appearances.

I said words to her that I'd never spoken aloud. I admitted feelings of betrayal, remorse, and loneliness, voicing them for the first time ever. I openly cried and wasn't a bit ashamed. She seized every opportunity to surreptitiously touch my hand or give it a gentle squeeze. We connected at levels far beyond the physical attraction. She had insights and a way of knowing me better than I knew myself.

Six weeks earlier her father had died from colon cancer after a courageous five-month battle. She was working through the grieving process in a healthy manner and was intuitive enough to express concern that I hadn't grieved for my father. Somehow she *knew* that sorrow had gone haywire inside me. She told me so in clear terms.

I listened, but not for the first or last time in our life together, I didn't hear what she was saying. It'd be easy to use the excuse that I was lost in her eyes because that was certainly true, but that'd be what used to be referred to as a cop-out. Reality was far more convoluted. Without even knowing it, I'd shut down the natural grieving mechanism. In time, comprehension would come, but then, while aimlessly shuffling cards, my inner workings seemed normal.

When the first camping session came to a close, Anita and I volunteered to be chaperons on the bus taking the children back to the city. It would give us a free day before we'd accompany the next group to Camp Brookhaven. We were young and reckless, set loose in the Big Apple. We left Friendship Chapel early in the morning to go sightseeing on, quite literally, a nickel and dime budget. The subway was an adventure that can still make us smile. We weren't sure where we were going or how to get there, and whatever noteworthy points of interest we may have seen along the way were unimportant. Talking, laughing, and holding hands, we were entirely oblivious to the bustle around us.

After making transfers and changing lines, we exited the subway at 57th Street at Broadway Avenue. We asked directions, then walked along Broadway, angling our way past vendors and street performers at Columbus Circle to arrive at Central Park. We walked all the way to the lake, then decided to look for the zoo, but after wandering around for a long while and seeing unsavory characters engaged in various illegal activities, we found a quiet spot to be alone.

The sun was at the top of an endlessly blue sky, and there was a gathering crowd of people in the park. We climbed on an outgrowth of rock, settled beside each other on a smooth spot, and sat in silence. So much had already been said. We knew secrets about each other to which no one else was privy.

It was there and then, sitting on those rocks, nine days after our first encounter, that I asked Anita Irene Whitesel to marry me. Her answer was immediate and affirmative, but even before the soft whisper reached my ears, her eyes sparkled their magic, and my heartbeat quickened. She quoted Ruth: "Where you go I will go, and where you stay I will stay. Your people will be my people and your God my God." I cried. She cried. And the rest of the day disappeared as we dreamed our dreams.

It wasn't long before the news of our engagement was all over town, or in this case, all through the camp and along family networks in two countries. There was much uproar from all quarters about us not even knowing each other and being too young and all of that, but we dismissed it. With thirty-plus years in the rear-view mirror and our fortieth anniversary on a near horizon, I'd have to say that true love proved all the naysayers wrong.

In late August, a year after that sun-kissed day in Central Park, I enrolled in Ontario Bible College. It was a big deal in our family. By now the expectations on me and for me were beyond control, but honestly, I had Anita on my mind more than anything else.

We'd been living out this fairy tale long-distance love story, with her in Pennsylvania and me in Ontario, which made life interesting, but never dulled the intensity of our feelings. There were wedding plans quietly taking shape that were projected a year or more into the future. We played along, but had developed an unwavering determination to start our life together. We joked about running off to get married, but we really thought those scenarios were impossible, though as days folded in on top of each other, we began to seriously contemplate this option.

I had debated and argued passionately to persuade counselors and the college administration to loosen their rules regarding incoming freshmen not being allowed to marry, but to no avail. We knew there would be consequences, though everything was being filtered through the fiery haze of our feelings.

Libraries are built around books filled with stories about the wonder and all-consuming nature of young love. Like so many factual and fictional couples, our romance was bigger than us, larger than the confines of our best intentions. We were caught up in each other, so as soon as we could coordinate our getaway plans, Anita and I eloped, which burned up telephone lines and set-off tremendous hand-wringing.

There's some dispute as to whether I dropped out or was kicked out of Ontario Bible College, but with the blood of stubborn people in my veins, along with being nineteen and full of myself at the time, it is fantasy to imagine me quitting. As I remember it, I forced the issue and was summarily expelled.

In all of this there's a point that cannot be missed. If I hadn't fractured my hip, and if my father had not been killed, I wouldn't have been on staff at Camp Brookhaven the summer of 1973. There would have been no way. My father was a practical and demanding man, and if the cruel accident hadn't befallen him, my summers would have been filled with work, hockey school, and preparation for college. Without the injury, more likely than not, I would have been pursuing the certification necessary to drive a dump truck.

Also, the death of Anita's father in May cracked open a door of opportunity that she'd never considered. Taking a break from her summer job to do ministry work wasn't even remotely in her plans. It was at the fellowship meal after the funeral that the camp director, a family friend and soon to be a brother-in-law once removed, planted the seed-idea with her. He told her that it'd be healthy to get away from routine and pour herself into children who dearly needed touches of grace.

From the example set by her parents, she understood that emotional well-being was closely connected to serving others, so the seed-idea fell on fertile soil. She mulled it over for a bit, then calculated her finances and arranged her schedule accordingly.

Evaluating these facts and seeking comprehension doesn't change the hard reality: Nothing fills the huge holes these good men left behind or diminishes the pain one iota. The sense of loss transcends generations, leaving its mark in ways that can't be easily categorized.

They never held a grandchild; none of their grandchildren ever got to know them, except in pictures and tall-tales, which are undeniably rich blessings. In the telling of stories the virtue of their character casts shadows that still have the power to influence us. The cliché that loved ones are never forgotten when their memory is kept alive is no cliché at all.

Roses coexist with thorns; pleasure is entwined with pain. Life is what it is, which is often difficult to grasp, but with hindsight being twenty-twenty, I can't help but be amazed at how God used the extremely hard stuff of life for his purposes.

Anita and I were created for each other, yet without the onset of tragedy, in all likelihood we would have never even met. Our lives came together in ways having nothing to do with the accumulation of coincidence. The results could only have been orchestrated by God, and since God doesn't shoot craps, there's no way to compute the immeasurable odds for our story.

Think it over: A young lady from Pennsylvania meets a young man from Ontario in upstate New York, and in a tender moment when they were totally alone in a roomful of people, their hearts became entangled, soon followed by the interlacing of their lives.

This causes me to ruminate on the bewildering marvel of life. How can we know what events are going to ultimately bring? The desperate chances, the diverse uncertainties, the disconnected fragments, the inconceivable accidents, and the incomprehensible diseases; how do these bits of life factor into the grand scheme? How do they become interlocked into the big picture? And when one considers the vastness of the past, with its myriad potentials and possibilities, it's only faith in God and the everlasting extravagance of grace that brings meaning to the transient and temporal nature of life here on planet earth.

The good, bad, and ugly are all elements in the spectrum, but while we're in the middle of the story, we can't know how each one will play itself out. We can't know how all the seemingly random vagaries will fit together.

Here's a mystifying nugget of truth: We're *always* in the middle of the story. The narrative is a portrait that's never fully finished because life isn't static. Our circumstances are like a jigsaw puzzle, which is always in flux, with the pieces being arranged on the board by the singular Cosmic mover and shaker. Only the Creator has the ability to take the tattered remnants of jagged-edged pieces and restore them so they slip easily into place beside smooth-edged ones. Even when we willfully disobey, God works things together, though it's only in the passage of time, coupled with generous wisdom from above, do we gain a semblance of discernment.

After my short stint in college, just long enough for a coffee and a donut, Anita and I sought refuge in each other. I wanted to escape from whatever was chasing me. I wanted to drop-kick responsibility into the bleacher seats. We became self-involved and eased away from church, beginning to sever relationships, yet in our self-absorption we couldn't elude the sovereignty of God, who was still actively positioning and using situations on the board of our lives.

In February 1976 we were living in Reebs Bay. We had a son, who'd been born in April 1975. He was named after my father, but following in the footsteps of the grandfather he'd never meet, he's always been known by his middle name. At times it can get confusing because it's the same as my first name.

I was working at Canadian Furnace in Port Colborne at the time. The plant, a division of Algoma Steel, was situated at the mouth of the Welland Canal on Lake Erie. It produced one product, pig-iron. The market for it was always volatile. This winter was a boom period. Overtime was free for the asking, so I was putting in lots of hours.

It was slugging grunt work that required nothing more than the proverbial strong back and weak mind. Arthritis had already begun to thread its way into the left hip joint, and all the heavy lifting exacerbated the chronic inflammation. It bothered me more and more, and it was in this time-frame as a steelworker that I began self-medicating for the pain, a practice which would get increasingly erratic and risky over the course of twenty-plus years.

Early one morning the phone rang. I wrapped a pillow around my head. Anita got up to answer it. In a bit, with more than a little irritation in her voice, she told me that it was for me. I muttered something un-intelligible, but she insisted in a tone that hinted at exasperation, which didn't seem to fit. The house was cold, with each wooden step groaning its complaint as I made my way downstairs.

"It's James," Anita said tersely. "He won't tell me what he wants."

I took the phone from her and grunted a hello.

"Lawrence was in an accident last night," my uncle said. "He's dead."

"What?" I replied, coming wide awake as my face twisted up.

"Lawrence, your cousin . . ."

"Yeah," I cut in, "I know who Lawrence is. What happened?"

"Car accident on Lakeshore Road near Long Beach," he answered, his voice tense and touchy. "It's bad, Kenny. Real bad. Lawrence isn't the only one dead."

When I hung up, I repeated the news to Anita, got dressed while she was busy with the baby, and left the house. I got in the car, keyed the ignition, and smoked a cigarette as the engine warmed up. I lit another off the smoldering ember of the first and just sat in the driveway, working junk through my head.

Lawrence was dead; my cousin had been killed; my friend was gone. He was less than a year my junior, and along with me, a charter member of the Nice-guy Delinquents. To the adults in our lives during our growing up years he was always known as Lawrence or Lawrie, but within that crew of pranksters, he was affectionately called by his last name, Major or just plain Maj.

There wasn't much we hadn't done together. We'd balanced each other out. I was careful, he was careless; I'd hedge my bets, he'd play it fast and loose even when he was holding nothing; I'd pussyfoot around the edges, he'd charge straight into a fracas. Maj had a razor sharp edge to him that I admired to the point of even attempting to emulate it, though seldom with any success. I was too level-headed. Being reasonable was my contribution to the relationship, though considering some of the disturbances we'd been in the middle of, apparently my voice of caution must not have been expressed too loudly. Either that or we simply ignored it.

Maj could talk his way in or out of trouble like no one else I've ever known. He had this impish twinkle in his dark eyes, which was constant, but he could always crank it up a little brighter as the need arose. That gleam in his eyes caused even the most hardened authority figure's mouth to crease into a smile as Maj explained away his attitude or actions. It happened more than once, and I should know because I was often the eyewitness melting down or freaking out beside him.

"No big whoop," he'd say, after extricating us from one jackpot or another. His assessment usually proved true, though there was once when a supposed *no big whoop* actually became a big whooping that turned itself into family folklore. We must have been nine or ten, young enough to be where we ought not be, and old enough to know there'd be trouble if we got caught.

It was late winter, early springtime; an interval that comes along every year when nature doesn't quite know how to act. Should it blow up a storm and bluster an arctic blast or would it be acceptable to warm up and spread sunshine? The weather pitches schizophrenic throes; summery one day, wintry the next. This day had brought a halt to the most recent thaw by doing a pretty convincing imitation of the dead of winter, with plenty of grayish ice shrouding ponds and ditches.

Maj and I had spent a good chunk of the morning tramping around the bush and quarry playing trailblazers. He was Davy Crockett, and I was Dan'l Boone. I didn't know it then, and it would be a shock when I found out, that the two pioneer heroes gained their reputations in completely different travels and adventures. But my cousin and I, along with millions of other television addicts, had been thoroughly *Disneyfied*.

We had broomstick long-rifles, and our coonskin caps were woolen toques knitted by Grandma Major. Purloined slats of snow-fence had been whittled into knives and tucked into our belts. We were double-socked and plastic-bagged inside our gum-rubber boots, and our hands were protected by thick mittens Grandma had fashioned out of old work socks. Queenie was with us, running hard and barking happily. She ranged ahead, darting one way, then the other.

Noontime was creeping up on us. Behind the leaden-hued cowl of clouds the sun was climbing high in the sky, and our stomachs were growling fiercely. We were traipsing across the quarry floor, pausing every thirty yards or so to bend low and get a reading on the imaginary tracks we were following, but the frontier illusion was beginning to lose its shine. We decided to head to his place and get some grub.

The quarry was the hole in the ground legacy of Canada Cement, who'd mined it for all it had to give, then abandoned it, which was good for us because it was the greatest playground ever. We climbed to the top of the jagged wall like a pair of mountain goats and congratulated ourselves on being sure-footed, then angled straight for his house, which would prove to be problematic. To get to his place from where we were in a direct line meant that we had to go across Wilverwild. It was a world-class frogging paradise when it was hot and sticky, and when the snow flew, it became one of the finest ice hockey rinks in the area. On this particular day we were both under orders to stay off the ice because it was thin and mushy. We had been read the riot act; we were not to go anywhere near Wilverwild.

Queenie came up behind us and scampered past onto the ice. She skidded sideways like she always did, but it hardly even slowed her. Before we stepped onto the frozen bog, she'd scooted off and up the bank on the other side, disappearing among the stringy vines of tangled brush and stark bare trees which stretched skyward like gnarled old fingers. We started across side by side, and it sounded like a bad movie soundtrack. Tiny pops and scratchy moans accompanied every step. We separated and spread out. Maj flipped his broomstick over and the long-rifle magically transformed into a hockey stick. He started stick-handling a phantom puck, and I quickly assumed the goalie's crouch as he barreled down on me. He took a mighty wind-up and let it fly. My right leg kicked out like a blur of lightning, then I was down covering the rebound.

Maj slouched against his stick. "This ice ain't bad."

He bounced up and down. The entire pond vibrated.

I took up his dance because it was humorous the way the ice roiled and had the elastic action of a trampoline. Each time we went up, we came down harder. We were laughing, shouting, and having a grand time because the ice was spongy and rippling. It was a sheet of rubber, and we were distracted by its shimmering recoil, so we didn't hear the cracking of its dying spasms.

Queenie must have heard them. She poked her head out of a clump of brush and bayed loudly. Her bull-throated notes raised ridges of gooseflesh on the nape of my neck. I glanced over at her, and it was then that it happened. Disaster struck. Her warning howls came a split-second too late. Maj and I were in perfect rhythm, and when we came down, there was a horrendous ripping explosion as the ice opened its maw to gobble us up. My stomach clenched, and I gasped in horror.

As luck would have it, my gasp came just as I went under the frigid water. It gushed into my lungs. My vision distorted, then blackened. The drumbeat of my heart throbbed in my ears. My feet hit the mushy bottom, and my knees buckled out from under me, but then I jack-in-the-boxed up and broke the surface, thrashing crazily. Maj was scrabbling belly-first out of the hole and I blindly followed his example. We wormed out of the muddy water and sprawled on the shore gulping and spitting. I felt sick. We looked at each other as our breathing settled to a near normal pattern.

"What are we going to do?" I asked, trembling.

"No big whoop," he answered, eyes narrowed. "We go to my place and hope my father's still at work." He stood and I shadowed him. True to character, he'd isolated the problem and hit the pay-dirt of a plan with the minimum of talk and effort. If his father was still at work, we had it made. Aunt Kay might yell at us and stir up a fuss, but that'd be all. She'd get us dried off and warmed up. But Uncle John? Or my Dad? We both knew what we were up against.

What happened then would likely be considered primitive or maybe even child abuse in some circles nowadays, but I'd never reach either of those conclusions. We merely got an old-fashioned spanking. Uncle John was home. He wasn't the sort of man to coddle disobedience, and we'd both been raised from the cradle to know that we were responsible for our actions. His investigation consisted of a quick once-over of our slimy condition, then he sat on a kitchen chair, bent Maj over a knee and delivered six solid whacks. I cringed as each blow hit the mark, getting the idea that now would be a good time to examine the floorboards. Then it was my turn.

I pinched my eyes shut to squeeze off the tears, but it didn't help. They worked their way out because his open-handed slaps on my buttocks stung like the dickens. When he finished, he stood us up in front of him and told us in no uncertain terms to go to my house. And just like that we were outside. He didn't give us a chance to dry off or warm up to the bone or nothing.

Once in our kitchen we received the exact same treatment from my father. The second whooping was a punctuation mark to teach us a lesson, which I'm sure was what Uncle John intended. In our family circles, as the years gave it some significance beyond all proportion, the story was told with much snickering and eye-rolling.

Someone even shared it at the funeral home, along with many other stories involving Maj. It was all quite disconcerting, and though friends and relatives were always around in the days following my cousin's death, I was alone and afraid. Violent death *was* stalking me. That thought carved itself so deep into my psyche that I believed it completely. I couldn't conceive of it not being true. Violent death *was* always lurking nearby. It was there on the fringe of my life waiting for the chance to crush me or bury me or trap me in the twisted steel of an automobile. I smoked like a fiend, unable to get enough nicotine into my bloodstream. I started drinking in binges and didn't care anything about it as I sorted through memories and scratched some down on paper.

I was not yet twenty-one years old. Dad, Uncle Frank, Peter, and now Maj. They were all dead and gone. In a short five year span they'd all been killed. Some of the details of each appalling accident were gruesome enough for grisly images to get stuck inside my head. A nauseating montage looped over and over in my mind as I stood beside another closed casket in the same funeral home on the corner of Clarence Street and Elm Street in Port Colborne.

I was traumatized by the raw hardness of this season of pain. Something was rapidly unraveling deep down in the core of me, and I didn't even try to stop it. Hidden in the shadows, everything necessary to rise above the heartaches was likely available, but in my state of mind, I don't think I wanted to find nor apply the tools to cope. Staring numbly at the snapshot of my Cousin Lawrence displayed on the coffin, a madness churned wildly in my soul.

All the years of pent up mourning shattered the natural release valve inside me. Grief geysered to the surface and crystallized itself into a fist-clenched rage at God: *How could God be so mean-spirited? How could he keep killing the people I loved?* The frenzied soliloquy ranted on while other mourners came to weep or pay their respects, but, immersed in an internalized belligerence, I took no notice.

After awhile, I went outside and hesitantly paced on the sidewalk. I was alone in the cool night air. My breath dispersed in shallow wisps as I vigorously stoked the bitterness and foul language directed at the One who had created me. Right there and then, while grinding my teeth and quietly cursing the moon and stars, I made a conscious choice to close myself off to God. I wanted nothing more to do with him. Emotionally, spiritually, and even physically I checked out, and in doing so, began a slow and steady descent into the depths of misery.

3

Season of Exile

"Then you will say in your heart, 'Who bore me these?
I was bereaved and barren; I was exiled and rejected.
Who brought these up? I was left all alone
but these—where have they come from?'"

~Isaiah~

WHAT RESULTS WHEN GOD'S love is rejected? Do consequences come when one spits at grace while choosing to cut loose from spiritual moorings? What happens when grief is submerged? These questions will be explored here. Be forewarned, what follows has elements of downright ugliness, but be assured that because *God's compassions never fail, he works everything together for his purposes*, so remarkably, while on a grief-stricken rush to personal disaster, grace held firm.

Grief is relentless. It can be a feral beast, spasmodically marking its territory with bursts of stinking secretions, which have the viral potency to distort and even destroy character. Loss and sorrow must be processed one way or another. When it's suppressed, it works itself out pathologically.

In this self-imposed exile, my well-practiced denial festered within me like an unlanced boil that continued to fill with poisonous pus. There's no point in attempting to sugarcoat it. In this season, I was a rotten father, a rotten husband, a rotten brother, a rotten son, a rotten friend, and generally speaking, an all-around rotten human being.

There was this toxic spill of wounds in my life that seeped into every nook and cranny, contaminating relationships and opportunities. It was all-encompassing. I developed a self-destructive, anti-social bend that isolated and alienated me from others. I took intentional steps to withdraw from society as much as possible.

My outlook was darkened by a fatalistic view which caused me to believe that a tragedy was waiting for me around each and every corner. It's impossible to emphasize enough the negative affect this fatalism had on me. It was a living thing gnawing away at my insides. My physical appearance became scraggly and unkempt, and my health rapidly deteriorated as I smoked, drank, and abused my body. I put on excessive weight because, after all, I had the attitude that nothing really mattered and so what if it did?

It was often scary for those closest to me. I was functionally dysfunctional and couldn't explain what was going on inside my head or how it was manifesting itself in my life. It was all so real, yet so incomprehensible and unreachable. I had monstrous mood swings, and it took all I had to just hang on and not let go. A large part of me was spinning out of control in a downward spiral, and I expected to crash and burn. At some junctures, I might have even wanted to crash and burn.

In my addled state, there was no future for me. My father had been killed, but there was more than that fouling up my brain. His father had been gruesomely injured in an explosion at a steel mill in Welland, dying an excruciating death before my second birthday. The contemporaneous newspaper accounts of that industrial accident harassed me, especially now, because I was employed as a steelworker and feared what was going to happen to me.

The messed-up maelstrom of my muddled thinking had some other bothersome tidbits of information to process. An uncle in his early twenties had been crushed to death at work before I was even born. Add in a great-grandfather killed in a train accident when he was young and healthy, and it's one helluva sinister family tradition that I viewed as inevitable.

My life was destined to end in the same sort of indiscriminate accident. I was going to die young, period. End of discussion. This acceptance of a pre-destined calamity screwed itself through me. The stone-cold sober idea that our bloodline was cursed slithered around the edges of my thinking. I was tormented by thoughts of a violent death for years and years. Menacing misgivings invaded my sleep. I would receive middle-of-the-night phone calls from my father sounding an alarm and wake up in a cold sweat, suffocating, and disoriented.

As far as church was concerned, I dropped off the face of the earth and deliberately broke away from that circle of friends. It was much more insidious than just desiring to be free of their expectations. I wanted to rip the Jesus vaccination out of my veins; I wanted to divest myself of any remnant of faith; I wanted to drown the call to pastoral ministry in a beer-soaked grave. A hot anger at God simmered inside me, and it was always extremely close to boiling over.

Even so, in a little twist of irony, I never stopped talking to him. I'd vent black-hearted thoughts; I'd furiously despise my life and tell him so in gut-level phrases not heard in any church-house. He *never* flinched. In my darkest, near suicidal hours, I kept up this antagonistic dialog with God, which, when one stops to contemplate it, is the essence of prayer, isn't it? To openly converse with God in unfettered honesty; to strip away the pretense of pretty sounding words; to come to the end of one's self and have nowhere else to go or hide; to end the religious masquerade and be naked before our Maker is what prayer is all about.

In a slightly deranged way, I became the consummate seeker. I was desperate to find something on which to cling. There had to be meaning in all the debris. With a doubt-ridden and confrontational mindset, I prospected the pages of the Bible. I spent years burrowing through the Hebraic wisdom literature, digging deepest in the Psalms of lament, for their fervency mirrored my sorrow.

Many times these dredging expeditions occurred under the influence of alcohol or, more frequently, during the morning after hang-dog period when the ache in my soul was accompanied by knife blades being sharpened behind my eyes. The writer's undisguised emotions carried weight that provided a grain of hope which at the time was the resource that buoyed me up and kept me putting one foot in front of the other.

Without knowing it, I embraced mourning. I read somber writers of poetry and fiction, joining them in an exploration of the broken darkness that's the norm in a fallen world. I listened to the blues with a peculiar intensity that remains undiminished to this day; folk-blues, country-blues or rock-blues. The genre didn't matter much as long as the melody and rhythm was matched to neatly painted word pictures or unique turns of phrase. Story-songs all about loss and loneliness make up the soundtrack of my life. Some people have been discombobulated by this eccentricity of mine, and more than once in my sojourn in holy huddles, I've run afoul of the religiously-correct police. I always attempt to be sensitive, but invariably must dismiss their protests or judgment simply because we all tend to put down what we don't understand.

Some of my richest spiritual experiences or best times of inspiration come while listening to sad songs. During the early morning hours in which I sorted through this truckload of stuff in my head, there was always some bluesy roots music playing in the background. Emmylou Harris happens to be singing a Dylan tune just now. And by way of confession, though maybe we ought to keep this just between us, but more often than not, for me sermon preparation requires an eclectic mix of Bob Dylan or Big John Cash to accentuate the process.

Some mental health survival instinct must have arbitrarily kicked in because, in searching for meaning by identifying with a literary landscape others would see as desolation personified, I wrapped sorrow and angst around me like a cloak, and in doing so, was grieving at some level. Being occupied by the fictional or real life heartaches and misery of others caused something mystical to begin taking place.

It would take years to be realized, and some more years to perceive it, but by the grace of God, all the piercing bitterness became a fertilizer with nourishing ingredients that permeated my soul.

Fertilizer can be just another word for cow manure, which is the nice way to refer to cow poop, and everyone knows that, regardless of what we call it, cow excrement has an overpowering acidic odor. Just so, while God was transforming grief and loss into a nutritious compost that eventually would allow something decent to grow, it reeked. More accurately, my response to accumulated pain stunk up my life big-time, yet even in this, God remained on the job.

By way of illustrating one way God was using everything to prepare me for his purposes, consider this: In 1978, on the day it arrived at the local record store, I purchased *Street Legal*, an album by Bob Dylan. I took it home where it remained on the turntable for weeks while I proceeded to listen to it until the grooves all but disappeared. It's a vastly underrated work, but perhaps that's merely my biased opinion. Due to some harsh economic realities combined with the transition from long-play vinyl to compact discs there was a period of fifteen years or so that I didn't have access to it. In 2004 I got the remastered CD, immediately rediscovering its brilliance that had almost been forgotten.

Its smoke and mirror imagery spoke anew to me. One day while driving alone with the volume cranked up so loud the speakers in the door were vibrating, I sang or shouted out the lines in an old familiar way. Lost inside the free association poetry, suddenly a lightbulb illuminated my brain. My voice went silent as I eased off the gas, turned the music down, and cracked a gigantic smile.

An epiphany that was instantaneously obvious to me caused me to laugh out loud. It came to me in a flash of perfect clarity. Dylan's writings are rooted in a postmodern worldview, with the lyrics of *Street Legal* put forward as prime examples. It could easily be argued that he was one of the original expositors of postmodernist musings. His body of work has intricately woven itself into my life, meaning that, as his music resonated with me, subconsciously it imbued me with an education in the whys and wherefores of postmodern abstractions.

I distinctly recall the moment Dylan's words first galvanized my imagination. It was September 1969. The ninth grade at E. L. Crossley Secondary School, with its different faces and experiences, was keeping me riddled with adolescent anxiety. The incessant pain in my left leg made the limp very pronounced, which targeted me for snide remarks and ridicule. Mix in the fact that acne had decided it'd be nice for me to start high school with a bumper crop of big juicy zits, and I was nearly inconsolable, a pimple-faced gimp lugging around self-defeating feelings of alienation and isolation. I had perfected being all alone in a crowd.

I was sequestered in that safe place within one afternoon, sitting beneath a tinny sounding speaker on bus number 18, when 1050 CHUM played *Like A Rolling Stone*. I'd learn later that it'd been on the scene since 1965, but it was brand new for me. From its opening gunshot drumbeat, the song skewered me. The cacophony of sound, followed by a voice saturated with attitude: "Once upon a time . . ."

Its twisting lyrical story had me completely under its spell. The cast of characters is bizarre; it includes jugglers, clowns, a diplomat, a Siamese cat and assorted pretty people. The hook-line question grabbed me and wouldn't let go. It was spat out with an audible sneer: "How does it feel?"

How does it feel? By the end of the six-minute record, I was possessed by a determination to know everything about the artist. In six minutes, a world of sheer fascination opened up, and my musical preferences had been settled.

When I came to ministry in the early 1990s, relating to the times in which we lived wasn't a challenge. While friends and colleagues who'd been schooled in seminary grappled to get a handle on it, I never had to jump through hoops or do mental gymnastics to understand postmodernist thinking. It came entirely naturally to me.

Who could know that a byproduct of a sometime obsession would be an ability to communicate my way through the postmodern maze? *All of life is preparation, so everything happens for a reason as God works everything together for his purposes.*

January 1980 found us living in Sault Ste. Marie, Ontario. Canada Furnace went belly-up, and the employees were given the option of transferring to the main Algoma Steel facility in the northern town referred to as the Soo, usually with some affection, though sometimes derogatorily.

We'd moved in the spring and summer of 1977, ostensibly to follow the job, but hidden in a secret cavern within where no one was ever allowed, escape was motivating me. Despite my outward expressions to the contrary, God hadn't abandoned me. He was, in fact, coming after me hard. I would never have framed it this way or even had the knowledge to ponder it then, but the theology of place was in play and having an influence on me. The Port Colborne BIC Church, the place of my primary spiritual experiences, was always there beside the highway to convict me.

When the offer of employment in a far-off city came, it seemed entirely reasonable to take advantage and break away from that ever-present building. If I could do so, perchance the discontent and inner nagging of guilt over wasting my life would magically fade into nothingness. As crazy as it seems, that idea was truly in my mind. Putting it in print now is an uncomfortable reminder of just how thoroughly misshapen my perspective had become.

As we examined alternatives, looked at logistical details, and worked through the whole concept of moving to Sault Ste. Marie, we had many conversations, and a particular one has stuck with me. It occurred in the living room of our house in Reebs Bay, with the morning sunshine streaming through the windows. Anita took a blade to remove the minutia and cut to a heart question.

"Are you really a steelworker?"

"I pay union dues, so I must be," was my flippant answer.

"So you want to make a career of it?"

"Not sure what you mean."

"If we move way up there, are you prepared to spend the rest of your life as a steelworker?" she asked, giving me a look that made me squirm.

There was a long silence while I mulled over a full range of potential replies, then, summoning all the trust that'd been built up between us, I stared into those sparkling eyes and gave her a direct response: "Yes."

There was just one tiny problem with my blunt answer. As I consciously pushed the full force of my personality at her, I was lying like a seasoned politician, and worse than that, I *knew* I was lying, and what was even more disturbing was the fact that I'd reached a point where I didn't care, which is a frightening place to be.

In that awful instant I completely betrayed myself, which became another shame-ridden rock in the dungeon I was busily erecting around me. Many years later, when those walls were crumbling down and there was much to deal with, I initiated a replay of that dialog, to acknowledge that I had willfully lied to her. She told me that I hadn't fooled her one bit; she'd known all along, but I was deceiving myself first, and until I ended that charade, she'd have to love me and wait it out. Go figure.

In January 1980, we had two boys. Our second son, Michael, had been born in April 1978. I was trying to be a devoted father, and sometimes I might have even had some success, though given my clogged up emotions, I'm not sure I would have recognized what success in that area would look like. I was too screwed up.

My sons were precious, and I had these high hopes for them, and I wanted to be a good father, but there were miles and miles between intent and action. I was calloused, hardnosed, and unresponsive. There was this sense of helplessness; it was like I was standing outside of myself watching this lunatic who was a replica of me, and I couldn't intervene to stop his absurdities.

Working on and around the blast furnace floor, with its overpowering heat and stench of sulfur, was a glimpse of hell or some type of purgatory. The danger to one's physical safety, regardless of protective apparel, training, and precautions, was always an imminent threat. The meaningless nature of the day to day shoveling or lifting crates or taking samples or diverting molten iron could be emotionally debilitating.

There was always this nagging sense in me that I was being pursued. My conscience couldn't be silenced, and from time to time, God would make his presence known. He kept placing Christ-followers in my circle of co-workers. I'd debate and argue theology with them, often taking great delight in unleashing a verbal pit bull to intimidate or bludgeon them into submission.

One particular guy named Greg kept coming back with a gentle grace that was disarming, which had the peculiar effect of infuriating and intriguing me all at the same time. I vacillated between wanting to work with him and wanting to slap that assured smile off his face.

During a slowdown period, when one of the furnaces was off-line for repairs and maintenance, we were partnered up for several days in a row, getting assigned to do a series of the dirtiest of dirty jobs. Between these, I dropped my defenses and shared some of my story, specifically talking about my previous intention to enter the ministry. He listened, grinning as though I was passing him little nuggets of gold.

After that conversation, we were down in a pit, cleaning up a spill of coke and iron ore pellets. This task was one to be avoided at all costs, but we drew the short straw, so we strapped hip-waders on and were hard at it, heaving each shovelful up and over a shoulder into the bin.

"Hey," he said with a grunt, "you're Jonah."

I began cussing him out with fevered eloquence, but stopped in mid-sentence. A burst of brightness penetrated me. My breath caught in my throat, and I stopped. I leaned against the dank wall, which continually wept rivulets, so my back was almost instantly soaked.

A fresh view of the surroundings made me sick to my stomach. We were in a concrete-lined hole twenty feet below the surface, standing knee-deep in filthy water. The place was slimy and claustrophobic, having all the charm one would associate with the innards of a whale.

"Jesus," I whispered, much more a prayer than a curse.

"Tell me this ain't the belly of a whale," Greg said redundantly.

An anger raged fiercely within as a thought struck me hard. *Not the belly of a whale. I'm trapped in the belly of a beast. And I put myself here.* The words formed before I could prevent them from taking shape. I hated them with a guttural hatred. I began working furiously, swearing each time the shovel swung upward.

The job got finished, but the imagery remained. It was a wild-eyed prophet taunting me with the truth, which enfolded me in an immobilizing despondency. I was draped in a constant melancholia and, behind those bleak curtains, thoughts of my impending doom copulated with self-pity to give birth to a swarming nest of snakes in my soul. Then something happened that'd let loose all those snakes, meaning that I withdrew deeper into myself and became progressively self-destructive.

To get the scope of it, I must backtrack a bit, and hope you're sticking with my storytelling. When we moved to the Soo in 1977, I went north early to work and find an apartment, while Anita stayed in Reebs Bay to pack the house and take care of all the relocation details.

At first I lived at the Beaver Hotel, which was convenient in that it was close to the main gate of the plant, and more importantly to me, just one flight of steps down from my room was the bar where I could drink myself to oblivion. That spring was a six-week lost weekend. I drank incessantly, more often than I can say, to the point of blacking out. I was a lovable and slobbering drunk.

My job site was this place of pitfalls and peril, yet many times I'd be hung-over or half-blitzed. I ascertained that the throb of a hangover could be avoided if one woke up drunk and immediately started drinking again. I was blind to the folly of it; either that or I was just devoid of feelings one way or another.

While riding up and down on this inebriated carrousel, I started working with a guy named Wilf. He was a joyful, carefree man just a couple years older than I. We were paired up. Over the course of several days our task was to remove heaps of slag out of sand trenches.

Between the grumbling grunts and joking around, while our rubber-soled work-boots smoked and smoldered, we connected. We gave the bosses memorable nicknames which developed into elaborate tales about them. His smile wrinkled and lit up his face, and he was always smiling about something or other. He enjoyed hearing or telling a good story, as did I, so we became natural entertainment for each other. Early in our relationship it became obvious that he didn't smoke nor drink. Neither did he use bad language.

Wilf was married to Liz. They lived on St. Joseph's Island, though he always referred to it simply as St. Joe's. He had an enigmatic quality about him in the sense that he embraced his Native Canadian roots while at the same time keeping his distance. He never wanted to talk about it, but it was apparent that he had this inner conflict going on.

In many ways he was a throw-back to a previous century when having the knowledge and skill to live off the land was a necessity. He was entirely at ease in the woods or on the water. He took great pride and pleasure in hunting and fishing, things which were also of interest to me. He had a common man decency and a straightforward manner that could be unsettling.

Once when I was near the bleary-eyed bottom of myself, he asked what I was trying to prove. There was no moralizing or condemnation, just a candid question, which, upon reflection, I couldn't answer.

When Anita and Kenny arrived in July, I was sober. We spent good chunks of the rest of that summer visiting Wilf and Liz at their home on Canoe Point Road. On our days off, Wilf and I would spend hours together on the water fishing and talking. It brought back good memories of the countless times spent in similar surroundings with my Dad or Maj.

Fishing had been an essential component of my growing up years. There wasn't a time I could recall when it hadn't been important to me. It was often pursued for no other reason than to have fun, but it had been a long, long time since I'd gone fishing. Sitting on a bridge or in a boat with Wilf, skewering big juicy night-crawlers to catch northern pikes or pickerels, stirred up all these happy thoughts in me, but I was afraid to feel them.

Our friendship developed over a period of time. Wilf had a unique charm when it came to leaving. He'd always say, *"Catch you later."* or *"Catch you on the other side."* His manner was so upbeat that when it came to parting company one was anxious for the *later* or *other side* to arrive.

We remained on the same crew at work for almost a year, then the job situation changed. He took an aptitude test and got on a track toward management, which was good for him, but it meant that our shifts were always out of sync. We started passing each other coming and going, and began the inevitable slide into an easy routine of hanging out with those on the same shift. We'd try to stay current, and on some occasions our days off would coincide and we'd be able to do something together, but mostly life happened, and we drifted apart.

Then in January 1980 my favorite football team, the Los Angeles Rams, were making a respectable run in the play-offs. I was scheduled to work the Sunday of the NFC Championship game, so to watch it, I had to switch with someone. I did so and worked the Saturday graveyard shift. Unknown to me when I made the change, I'd be on the same furnace as Wilf. We didn't actually work together because he was busy reading gas meters and temperature gages while I spent most of the night in an overhead crane.

When *Quit O'clock* came around, we sat at our lockers talking football, hockey and catching up. I was already showered and dressed, but he was taking his time getting out of his grubby clothes. We shared a couple funny stories and had a good laugh, then I got up to go and told him I'd give him a call during the game. He nodded. When I got to the top of the stairs, I turned back just as he was walking into the shower room.

"See you later, man."

"Goodbye," he answered, shooting me a smile and a wave.

Outside, that word *goodbye* roiled through my head, striking me as weird. I tightened up the collar of my parka as a chill tickled up my spine, which had nothing to do with the sub-zero weather, with its biting wind-chill. My mouth puckered and I paused for a fleeting moment, but being exhausted and wanting nothing more than a few hours of sleep in a warm bed, I dismissed it and started hoofing it toward the gate. Later that morning, comprehension would mushroom up in me with a startling directness.

Back then, whenever I worked midnights, sleep deprivation was the norm. I'd get home shortly before seven-thirty and go straight to bed, and be lucky if I wasn't wide awake and up for the day before high-noon. Nothing I ever tried to do to get rest helped. I'd always tell Anita not to wake me unless the house was on fire. That morning she shook me awake before eleven, her face encompassed by concern.

"You need to come to the phone," she said, tears on her cheeks.

I reacted in silence, reading her like a book. I got up, stumbled out to the kitchen, and sat down when I picked up the receiver. "What?"

"Ken, Wilf was killed in a car accident on the way home this morning."

"No," I gasped, unbelieving. I asked several pertinent questions and got all the information available, then hung up and looked at Anita. "Wilf is dead."

"I know."

I remembered. The word *goodbye* flared up and exploded in me. I slumped forward. "He said goodbye . . . he said goodbye. He never said goodbye . . ."

"What?"

"It was creepy. Something was creepy, and that was it."

"What?" she repeated, her eyes full of hurt and worry.

I told her about his last word to me and the wave. "He knew." Then I swore with certain vehemence, solemnly cursing death and cursing friendship. I stared angrily at Anita. "God gave him a *two-minute warning*, and he knew he was going to die," I said adamantly. She reached out to me, but I pushed her away and slipped into a place of shadows inside to poke and probe that thought, turning it over and over to examine it from many different angles. The whole concept of God granting a death premonition remains capable of engaging my brain for hours at a time.

The funeral plans were finalized. Liz asked me to be a pallbearer. I really wanted nothing to with the job, but loyalty and honor compelled me. It was a most difficult task. The cemetery on St. Joseph's Island was a remote place. His grave was near the top of a little knoll in the shadow of some tall evergreens.

When the time came, gripped by the severe cold of a northern Ontario winter, the minister kept stamping his feet as he delivered the ashes to ashes graveside ritual, then it was the pallbearers' responsibility to lower the casket into the ground. We used long yellow straps, paying them out slowly and cautiously until the weight on them relaxed. Peering into that six-foot deep hole with the shiny box containing my friend settled at the bottom eviscerated me.

In the aftermath of Wilf's death, a few things occurred, one immediately and two others that ripened on a poison vine over the course of time. The afternoon and evening after the funeral I went into a bottle of scotch accompanied by beer chasers, and with few exceptions stayed in an alcoholic fog for several months. The snakes were loose, and killing or at least numbing them became a priority for me.

Also, fishing lost all its charm for me. Since Wilf's death I've gone fishing only prompted by family expectations and never enjoyed it again, even coming to despise it. And to this day, when someone says *good-bye*, I remember, and a part of me cringes. I usually urge them to say *see you later* or some other much less final farewell.

That winter and spring, sobriety and I became distant strangers. We didn't even have a nodding acquaintance with each other. Drinking and smoking was my chosen avocation, which I indulged without restraint or hesitation. There were likely some tobacco farmers whom I kept in business because I smoked incessantly. Cigars, cigarettes, or pipes, it didn't matter. Any and all forms of nicotine delivery systems were put to full use. The only time I breathed uncontaminated air was when I was sleeping. An ugliness had sank its hooks into me, and I was flailing around, lashing out in wild abandon, damaging body and soul, and harming those who loved me.

It was truly a wonder that Anita didn't choose to pack up our boys and leave me. Quite frankly, it may have been even more astonishing that she didn't take a gun out and shoot me dead, which, given her upraising in Pennsylvania where she reputedly was a hawk-eye shot, was always a possibility. She's the toughest person I've ever known, with a fierce love that confronted my particular brand of insanity with patience, grace, wisdom, and an unspoken challenge.

People on the outside looking in think that I'm the strong one, but they're completely mistaken. In our relationship, compared to Anita's determination, my character has the consistency of Jell-O. Exhibit A of her uncompromising tenacity would be how she responded to my headlong rush toward an alcoholic abyss.

When spring was blending into summer in 1980, at a stag for a friend who was getting married, I went on a binge that scared me. I woke up from it in our bed, but had no inkling of how I'd gotten home. Looking in the mirror, my face was blotchy and covered with dozens of little red spider-webs. My bloodshot eyes were swollen into mere slits. I stared at my reflection for several minutes and actually wondered who was squinting back at me. My mouth tasted like I'd licked a toilet bowl clean, which apparently, while heaving up loads of vomit, I'd come close to doing.

Anita didn't chastise or scold me at all. Maybe she should have hit me over the head with a frying pan, but she did no such thing. She nursed and cared for me with a tenderness that defied reason. In the wake of the frightening blacked out spots of that drunk, I began to deliberately ease away from the bars and bottles.

Shortly after that incident, we moved from an apartment to a three-bedroom duplex across town. Anita seems to have an innate gift for turning the empty spaces of a new place to live into a home full of warmth and security. After getting all the boxes and furniture into the house, she made her plans, then worked away at it. Each time I returned from work or wherever, there were new flourishes or touches to the layout and decor.

One afternoon she met me at the back door with one of those spar-kly-eyed smiles that can turn me into a blubbering idiot. She took me by the hand, telling me she had something to show me, then led me up-stairs. I could hear the boys in their bedroom giggling about something. In the hallway, Anita pointed to the closed door of the spare bedroom.

"Open it," she said, her face shining.

"What's going on?"

"Open it," she insisted, which initiated loud laughter from our sons.

"Okay."

I turned the knob and pushed the door open, stopping cold. My eyes couldn't translate all that was there to my brain. I leaned against the doorframe and shook my head in disbelief. I looked at Anita. She was crying through a smile that epitomized unconditional encouragement. My tongue chased over my lips and began to wrap itself around some words, but couldn't do it. I tried to speak several times, but for one of the few times in my life, I was speechless.

Sweet silence passed between us. And in the fullness of that silence much was communicated. She never had to express it in words because I received the message loud and clear.

From our earliest sharing with each other, she knew that I was a storyteller who aspired to be a writer. I'd conjure up plots for novels and provide intricate details that she'd listen to and say how interesting they were, and that I should write them down and make an effort to develop them.

Even though I hadn't purposely marked up any clean paper in years, evidently I talked about writing all the time, and so this woman who loved me and saw something in me that I couldn't find for myself, had transformed the spare bedroom into a den. By doing so, in her firm and resolute manner, Anita was telling me to put up or shut up. She was laying down a gauntlet, daring me to stop dreaming about it and start writing.

Now, I had to ante up, kick in, and be a man. I moved rubbery-legged into the room and sat down. I still couldn't believe what was sit-ting on the desk. By today's streamlined standards, it was a big green monstrosity, but to me, it was one of the most thrilling things I've ever seen. It was a commercial manual Remington typewriter destined to become a bossy teacher and tyrannical disciplinarian. It had a merciless quality and could stir anger up in me because it never allowed me to get the pictures onto paper as clearly as I could see them in my head.

I'd bang out words in frenzies of inspiration, but dissatisfaction with the results would make me nearly neurotic about rewriting. Those keys stayed with me and could take a beating without whines or complaints. I dearly wish I still had it on a shelf in my office as a touchstone, but in all the changes and rambling, it got left behind somewhere along the way.

I sat at the desk, with my hands fingering the keys. My mind was a jumbled mess. I kept looking around, amazed at her attention to detail. She hadn't missed a thing. There were paper clips, pens, yellow legal pads, and a ream of white paper. There was a dictionary, a thesaurus, and a Bible. There was special artwork. There was even the current book I was reading on an end table, along with the latest issue of *The Sporting News*. There could be no misunderstanding her intent; this was my room in which to focus on writing.

I was trying to fathom all that Anita had taken upon herself to do, trying to comprehend what she wanted or expected from me. Yes, I was definitely capable of doing lots of big talking about writing this or writing that, but it was always in grand abstract terms. We had never discussed any idea that would've been even remotely related to private quarters designed specifically for me to write. This was something born entirely in her heart. Her planning had to be thorough because this labor of love hadn't been accomplished in a day or two. I couldn't figure out how she'd kept all her preparations from me. Or how she'd managed to convince our sons to keep the secret.

"How? Why?" I finally asked in a scratchy whisper.

"I love you," was all she ever said. Then she left, closing the door behind her.

Alone in my room—my office—I soon realized that creativity doesn't run on an assembly line or by the dictates of the time clock. I picked up a piece of paper, and hesitantly fed it into that typewriter and lined it up. Swallowing hard, I put my fingers on the home-row.

I took a deep breath and thought about what to write. Nothing came to mind. I stared at the blank page for awhile, not exactly sure how one starts to produce a great novel. I clicked my teeth, sighed, and smiled as an idea popped into my head. I wiggled my fingers, drew another deep breath, then tapped out a sentence learned as a limbering up exercise in ninth grade typing class: *Now is the time for all good men to come to the aid of the party.*

It flew off my fingers with surprising ease. Of course it wasn't the opening line for any literary work, great or otherwise, but I was impressed that I could still make the keys do what I wanted them to do. I hadn't typed a single word in better than five years.

Just to make sure the effort wasn't a fluke, I returned the carriage and hammered out the sentence a second time. Then a third and fourth time. A rhythm developed, and a chuckle built up deep in my throat. I let it out with a burst, sat back, and recalled why I'd even enrolled in typing class.

Somewhere in my mind, there may have been some long-term thinking about learning a marketable skill, but I highly doubt it. In the eighth grade I'd discovered girls, so while looking at the alternatives for the high school freshmen schedule of classes, what was most important to me was the company I'd be keeping. At that time, it was almost an automatic that girls took typing, and since hanging out with girls was motivating me, my choice was something of a no-brainer.

There was a certain dark-haired girl who convinced me that typing class was the place to be by simply telling me that it'd be a lot of fun. I'd known her since the first grade, and family lore claims that I came home on day-one of school smitten by her. I don't know much about that; I do know that she was always a good friend and a highly sought after euchre partner.

It's interesting to note that God made allowance for all the normal quirks of adolescence and shaped them for his purposes.

Writing would've taken me to unknown levels of frustration if I had never learned to type. As it was, writing was fraught with discouragements, which, over the years, I'd probe with an unparalleled energy, never determining if having a way with words was a blessing or a curse.

While I sat in my new office that afternoon repeatedly typing gibberish, neither Anita nor I could've known how demanding writing would become or how obsessive I'd be about it, though it's clear that writing was a soul preserver. It kept me afloat. More than that, it gave me a sense of purpose and identity. By making all her plans and putting the whole notion of writing on the table as a viable option, Anita rescued me.

Looking back, it's easy to see that what actually happened was that, instead of trying to kill or numb the snakes by submerging them in alcohol, I was now going to stir up the nest and execute them one by one by writing them to death. Working on all this now, I must tell you that there's a few that have not yet been exterminated.

When the worldwide economic malaise of the early nineteen eighties hit the steel industry, Algoma Steel, the economic engine of Sault Ste. Marie misfired badly. I got a pink slip along with thousands of other employees. The lay-off didn't take me by surprise; I'd seen it coming, but not the depth or repercussions from it.

When I punched my timecard out the last time, I was grateful to be free of the place. It hadn't been a death-trap for me, but during my employment, there'd been numerous fatal industrial accidents, which intensified the twisted belief that a horrible death was stalking me, and I was fixing to die.

In a troubling stretch one August, the violent deaths at the plant occurred in such rapid succession that the news reports accompanied by my overpowering fatalism infected Anita. She was afraid for me. I could see it in her eyes and hear it in her voice. She greeted the job loss with relief mixed with a quiet faith that everything would be fine.

We couldn't know that my incarnation as a steelworker would be the last good-paying job with benefits that I would have for almost twenty years. Getting the heave-ho from the steel mill was an escape for me, but it also set off a long cycle of unemployment and underemployment that mercilessly chiseled away to embitter me. Applying for jobs and filling out the necessary forms became something of a joke, but no one was laughing. It was far too difficult to see humor in any of it.

Every week I pounded the pavement and knocked on doors in search of any kind of employment. There were under the table day-jobs that came along from time to time, so I'd dig a ditch or unload a truck or move furniture or get by doing some other mindless grunt work. The cash would be spent before it was in my hand because there were always bills to pay or groceries to buy. We scraped by, but my inability to provide for my family annihilated any vestige of a positive self-image that may have still lingered.

When I didn't have a job, which was more often than I care to remember, I pursued something for which I apparently had a natural flair. I wrote and wrote and wrote in a burning mania that gave fresh meaning to the word fanatic. Sunrise to sunset and often in the middle of the night,

I'd be perched in front of my typewriter, fiendish in my compulsion to get each sentence exactly as I could see it unfolding inside my head.

I tapped out page after page of what some would refer to as depressing poetry. It was bad poetry, to be sure, but depressing is a subjective judgment. Sorting through the layers of garbage in my soul to uncover words or phrases to be lined out in rhymes became daily prayer, though I never recognized it as that then.

The poetry had no particular significance for me beyond feeding an inner hunger that could never be satisfied. It always expected much more, and by providing nourishment, I was unknowingly engaged in an exorcism of sorts. Writing kept me alive; writing kept me tethered to sanity.

Once set free, my creativity's voracious quality constantly put me on edge. It was as though my imagination was jacked-up on amphetamines. Ideas came from nowhere; characters, plots and titles for stories were in plain sight everywhere I looked and materialized so rapidly I couldn't get them written down fast enough. I pumped out six or seven full-length novels, most of which were of dubious content, but a couple are likely worth revisiting and reshaping. In the writing and rewriting, I developed into a writer, and in the process, gained enormous respect for the craft.

However, in the marketing, I almost lost myself. If I had kept them on file, I could wallpaper a rather large room with the hundreds and hundreds of rejection letters. The business of writing remains a mystifying maze, and there are no maps available to warn of wrong turns or blind alleys.

That aspect of it can be the catalyst for confrontational moments with God in which I question whether writing is a gift to be treasured or penance to be endured. If nothing else, writing tempered me. God used it as a kiln to forge a perseverance in me that refuses defeat. After all, as one of my characters once quipped, "Someone has to tilt at windmills."

In March 1985 Grandma Major died. I was adrift inside the belly of a beast that had swallowed me whole and was actively digesting me. Whether I would ever make it out alive was a chancy proposition. Hunkered down in a basement bunker of an office, I wrote with a crazed desperation.

We were living in Welland, Ontario. We'd moved there in the spring of 1983 when it was clear that a recall from Algoma Steel wasn't even a remote possibility.

By this time, we had four sons. Wesley had been born in January 1981. We brought him home from the hospital on the day Ronald Reagan was inaugurated, and fifty-two American hostages were released from Iran. Our youngest, Jonathan, was born in April 1983, one year after the steel plant informed me that my services would no longer be required.

I remained earnest and deliberate in my efforts to be a decent father, but my love-hate relationship with God was steeped in ambiguity that kept everything in an unbalanced state. By this point, no matter what I did or didn't physically do, it always felt like there was a hot wire in the left hip joint, which stitched itself down the leg and across the small of my back. The pain management plan consisted of me regularly using a heating pad while eating over-the-counter extra-strength pain medication as though it was candy-coated bits of licorice.

We'd go for long walks together as a family, and whenever we'd stop to rest or skip rocks at the Welland Canal, I'd tell stories, many of which I'd heard from my grandmother, though in my telling they were tinged with a bleak outlook.

Grandma was by far the greatest storyteller I've ever known. A pastor once remarked that "Geraldine could talk the leg off the Lamb of God." I'm not sure what that means, but I can assure you that my grandmother had no difficulty keeping an audience enthralled. She'd draw the suspense out in even the most mundane or everyday stories.

While talking, her hands were never idle. In the summertime, she'd be busy snapping beans or preparing preserves; in the winter, she'd be sitting in her chair beside the floor furnace in the living room braiding a rug while spinning a real or imagined tale. Her grasp on facts was firm, but it's possible that her embellishment of an event might obscure the line between real and imagined. I dearly wish I would have recorded some of her stories. As an oral historian and pruner of genealogical branches, she was beyond peer.

Some favorite memories are tied into Saturday night rituals, which would be renewed each year when bitter winds tried to creep in out of the cold. In the sixties, Saturday night in the winter, meant family and hockey. Specifically, *Hockey Night In Canada*, with its distinctive theme song which was the unofficial national anthem, and whose iconic play-by-play man approached the status of an influential religious figure.

On many of those nights, I'd hang out at Grandpa and Grandma's house. Maj would be there, too, and we'd sit on the floor, watching the game while Grandpa carried on expert color commentary in the dead-air spaces between Grandma's stories. She would hold us spellbound, weaving our lives into the narrative with tidbits of information about this relative or that relative.

Grandma had what I would learn was a heightened awareness of the spiritual realm. Her faith in the God of the Bible was settled and unshakable, but when it came to matters of life and death, where one ended and the other began was open to interpretation for her.

Quite often an ordinary story would be progressing along in a usual way when suddenly she'd blend the supernatural in with a casual ease that made it all seem entirely natural. There was never any fear in her voice, but rather, always an awe and calm assurance, especially when the details got dicey or scary.

Without even being aware of it, she'd give us a bad case of the willies, which, in a single sentence delivered in hushed sincerity, could develop into a shivery outbreak of the heebie jeebies. On many of those nights, though the porch lights were on at both places, the fifty yard walk across back yards to my house was done so under extreme duress, with every shadow looking like a ghost.

On rare occasions, a particularly far-fetched story would cause Maj or I to wrinkle up our brow and ask, "Grandma, did that really happen?"

Her reply was quick and adamant. "Of course it did. Every word of it."

We'd look to Grandpa for further confirmation. He'd shrug, make this little click-click sound with his mouth, then say, "Grandma wouldn't lie, would she?"

Evidently not, but were there instances when fact and fiction got a bit distorted? For example, did a great-grandfather really return home for a short visit on the day he was buried because he'd forgotten to take something with him?

Those certainly are intriguing questions for which I can't provide a definitive answer. I can say without reservation that my grandmother was a truth-teller of the highest caliber. If you'd ever had an opportunity to hear her tell even the most eerie story, you'd know as I do that she was convinced every part of it truly occurred.

Grandma and Grandpa had more influence on my life than either of them ever knew this side of eternity. Most of my theology comes directly from them. Forget all the courses taken, books read, and endless philosophical discussions about the finer points of this or that doctrine. Before I was ten years old, my grandparents had taught me everything required to be an effective Christian. They did so with the integrity of their lives. They weren't saints, nor did they pretend to be; they simply believed what they said they believed, and fervently made every effort to apply their faith to their day by day lives, regardless of the circumstances.

The hymn *Make Me A Blessing* would surely be considered the theme prayer of their lives. Its lines are jam-packed with a practical theology that, if it were actually implemented on a large scale, Sunday mornings would find churches more overcrowded than the local mall with its cathedrals of commerce. And there would be far less greed and human suffering on planet earth.

I spent a large chunk of the summer of 1963 with my grandparents at Camp Kahquah, a sprawling campus of breathtaking solitude situated on a gentle hillside along Ahmic Lake near Magnetewan in northern Ontario. One had to be eight years old to be a camper, and since I didn't turn that magic age until October, I simply tagged along with them.

They were there as servants of the church, which I suppose didn't mean much to me then, but looking back at their example, always challenges me. Grandma was the cook, while Grandpa, being a handyman, took charge of the caretaker responsibilities.

The campground was a place of endless adventure for a boy with a streak of curiosity. There were well-laid out trails to follow, archery skills to be acquired, wood to chop, horses to ride and enough opportunities for mischief to keep me and my imagination busy. Queenie wasn't along, so there were times when I missed her terribly, but I had fun just the same.

One early in the season restriction sticks in my mind. In the roped off swimming area at the beach I wasn't allowed beyond the blue buoys because I hadn't demonstrated the necessary ability yet. By the end of the summer I passed the swimming test and was entirely pleased with my achievement.

In a natural landscape shared with hundreds of chipmunks and other wildlife, I learned an important life-lesson that became foundational to my comprehension of who God is and who I am. Much of my perspective of the world around me has its roots in an incident that occurred late one afternoon in a place surrounded by towering evergreens.

Grandpa and I were fishing off the end of the dock, which in those days was quite rewarding. The fish always seemed to be biting, and we'd catch our fill of perch and black bass in no time at all. The sky was gray streaks gathering together in big swirls, and there was a queer kind of color shaping up behind the clouds. I knew that because Grandpa said so.

"That's a queer kind of color, ain't it?" He made that habitual little click-click sound with his mouth while staring skyward. I followed his eyes and focused on it for a few minutes, amazed that the colors were constantly changing, which struck me as being pretty neat. Grandpa kept watching it, his eyes darting across the horizon every minute or so. The air started moving in off the lake. It felt like a warm and lazy breeze, but my grandfather stopped what he was doing, knelt and closed the tackle box.

"We'd better pack up, Kenny," he said, something funny in his voice.

"What's wrong, Grandpa?"

"Oh, nothing," he answered. "Let's get going."

I frowned, jiggling my line. All of a sudden the wind whipped up into a big whooshing gust, which caused the temperature to drop perceptibly. It came about so quickly that the nape of my neck prickled, and I scrunched up my shoulders as I hurried with my reel. Grandpa was all business as he grabbed our gear. The gray-streaked sky with its queer colors blackened almost instantaneously.

Flashes of lightning danced and crackled, and the lake began churning as though there was fire beneath it, causing it to come to a boil. It had happened so fast; one moment the surface of the lake was as calm as calm could be, rippled only by our bobbers. We had been joking around and teasing each other about whose fish was the biggest one caught. Then in the time it took a seven-year-old to reel in his line, we were racing away from cross currents of waves splashing over the dock.

Grandpa was hustling me along when a bolt of lightning slashed from the sky, accompanied by a clap of deafening thunder. It must have struck the ground near us or the water just behind us because it was bone-jarring, and in a split second there was an intense burnt odor in the air. I jumped. Well, that's likely a grand understatement.

What really happened was that I almost came out of my skin. A petrified scream ripped itself from my throat, and I couldn't breathe. When my feet came down, they were running, and they weren't going to stop until safety from the storm was found. I'd dropped my pole and whatever else I had in my hands and was halfway up the hill before I realized it. Another crash of lighting and thunder struck seemingly just as close as the earlier one. My legs were pumping faster and faster. I stumbled without ever slowing.

On the outside edge of control, I dashed into the cabin, almost knocking Grandma down as I scrambled to my room, where I cowered in a corner. In later years I'd refer to that thunderstorm as apocalyptic.

Just then, I was about to tap into a rich vein of homespun wisdom. Grandma came and picked me up. I was crying and she hushed me, telling me not to worry. She carried me out onto the porch. I squirmed and protested, but she insisted. She sat on the hanging swing, and I snuggled in beside her under the protection of her enfolded arms. It was cold and pouring rain now. The wind was blowing hard, and every few minutes a jagged flash of lightning was followed by a roll of thunder. In fact, to my ears, the rumbling was non-stop.

"There's nothing to be afraid of, Kenny."

I whimpered or whined something unintelligible, pressing in closer to her.

"It's nothing but a little storm," she said, rocking gently back and forth. "God is in complete control. He's showing us who's in charge of the world. And believe you me, this thunderstorm is just a tiny display of his power." She held her thumb and forefinger up to indicate a fraction of an inch. "This is God's creation. He's far more powerful than all the thunder and lightning in the whole world." Then she spontaneously broke into song: *"This is my Father's world, O let me ne'er forget that though the wrong seems oft so strong, God is the Ruler yet . . ."* Grandpa came along and joined in, their voices blending in harmony until the last words trailed off.

"That's fine singing," Grandpa remarked, smiling down at me as he patted my back. "Kenny, we almost got cooked out there, didn't we?"

"Percy, don't scare the lad," Grandma said, a mild rebuke in her voice.

I piped up, "I'm not scared anymore, Grandma." And I wasn't. The fear had dissipated, gone to wherever it is that fear goes when it runs away to hide. It was a settled matter for me. The omnipotence and sovereignty of God to a little boy was a profoundly simple fact: God was in charge of the world, and he was mightier than all the thunder and lightning I could ever imagine. The three of us sat on the porch watching the clouds sweep overhead as the storm huffed and puffed itself out. I've had an abiding appreciation for thunderstorms ever since.

Another lesson my grandparents taught me was one that occurred by osmosis over the years. Oakwood Cemetery forms one of the boundaries of Reebs Bay. It sprawls alongside Lakeshore Road across from Scout Point, and back then, it was gobbling up the land of the abandoned Boy Scout camp. My father referred to it as the marble orchard, and when the fish weren't biting, he'd vaguely crack-wise about the fish being skittish because the spooks were out and about. There are many relatives, both close and distant, buried there, which was the source for experiences filled with folklore and legends that inched perilously close to family mythology.

Every couple weeks or so each spring, summer, and autumn, various pairings of grandchildren would be recruited to go for a walk to the cemetery with Grandpa and Grandma. These were Saturday afternoon excursions, and as I recall, there was often jockeying among the cousins as to whose turn it was to be included. These were special times worthy of scraps with siblings to be the one chosen to tag along. The hike wasn't far, but it seemed like so much happened along the way. In the springtime, there were butterflies to chase and daffodils to pick; in the fall, we'd collect acorns or uniquely colored leaves.

Small gardening tools were brought along on every trip. We'd be assigned specific tasks to be carried out with great care. Fooling around in the cemetery was strictly forbidden under penalty of being banished from the crew. Any kind of infraction could get one banned from being selected for a long while, which kept us mindful of our behavior. We were regularly informed that life was precious, and since we were above ground, we were required to respect those whose bodies had been placed beneath the sod.

As I grew older, I discovered that the jobs we'd do had a soothing quality which couldn't be qualified or easily explained. There was planting or watering flowers, weeding, or generally tidying up the graves. All the while, Grandpa and Grandma would talk about each person's life, sometimes with laughter and sometimes with silent tears, depending on the story being told.

Much personal history was learned on these almost sacramental outings, but the lesson being instilled in me was an aspect of theology that became elemental. Life is short, and eternity is long, so being in the right place spiritually is the most important factor of life. That truth has no mercy or loopholes. It wouldn't relent or release me when I was making choices to escape or prove it wrong.

When my lifestyle was in self-destruct mode, Grandma never once served up condemnation. She provided love and acceptance. Her view was that the road was long with many twists and turns; the hard realities of life must have made her wise to the ways of wanderers. No matter my mood or frame of mind, I could always be encouraged having a cup of tea with her because she embodied grace, hanging onto it with a helpless determination. That knowledge came over time as she packed all the difficult real-life matters of the heart into her unyielding faith in God. Likely much of her assurance was the result of spending time contemplating life from the objectivity of a cemetery. She understood what it meant to number her days.

There's nothing like being in a graveyard. Having a comprehension of one's mortality is essential for purpose to be realized. I love graveyards. I've learned to seek them out wherever I am and walk through them often. There's solitude to be found among the stones marking the passage of life. There are untold stories to be considered while reviewing the chiseled names and dates.

Hopes and failed chances along with plans and high achievements are mingled in with the skeletal remains rotting in their satin-lined boxes and concrete crypts. In a world where happiness is an elusive commodity even though it's guaranteed in sixty-second commercials, time spent in a city of the dead keeps me focused on the fragility of life and the mystery of eternity. For me, they're places of extreme tranquility, and I have my grandparents to thank for that healthy perspective.

When Grandma's earthly life came to a close, I was nowhere near any place that resembled tranquility, let alone the extreme version of it. I was messed up and wallowing around in exile. Regrets can be ugly things that crawl up inside, latch on with leech-like tenacity, and can't be removed.

Sometimes God grants opportunity to fix mistakes or rebuild bridges we've burned, but often, those opportunities never materialize or we outright miss them. When that occurs, we have to deal with weighted feelings that are like an itch which can't be reached.

Grandma died after a long struggle. I had more than one chance to come to my senses while she was still alive, but somehow couldn't or wouldn't put into practice precepts she'd modeled. She never knew that, by God's grace, I emerged from my dark and lonely quagmire, so on occasion, pangs of remorse can still nip at me, but there's comfort knowing she never stopped hoping or praying for me.

Grandma's declining health was painful to watch. I was in my thirtieth year, and it was my first exposure to the death of a loved one by natural causes. She'd had a stroke and was partially paralyzed. She couldn't talk. Her eyes were bright and full of expression, but the wiring between her brain and tongue was frayed or had been short-circuited. The best she could manage was an insistent, "I want that."

Here was this exceptional spinner of stories rendered speechless, which made no sense whatsoever. In my mind, this was another example of God's mean-spirited nature, which only proves self-deception had me determined to use every and any circumstance to hurl epithets at the One chasing me down.

For everyone who had eyes to see, my grandparents taught lessons about the meaning of love. Grandpa cared for her every need with tender compassion. For Grandma, there were times of unmitigated frustration with her inability to speak, but mostly she exhibited gracious acceptance of her lot. If bitterness ever crept in for either of them, they'd lift each other out of it with some good-natured teasing. In that department, they were both capable givers and takers, which was the full flower of a love that had grown together for over half a century.

There were times when being the primary caregiver frazzled Grandpa, but no one ever heard him complain. Exhaustion was evident in the lines of his face and tone of his voice, but no matter how tired he became, he refused any and all efforts to put the love of his life into a nursing home. His children pushed him hard to do so, but he'd get indignant or stubborn about it, saying, "After all the good years Mom and I had together, how could I ever do that to her?"

Those weren't idle words. Neither was it rose-colored glasses talk because they'd had their full share of difficulties and hardships. Some of the stories that'd been told were layered by hurt and disappointment, and I'm sure they had their struggles with each other. Their relationship most certainly had heartaches and heartbreaks, but the sincerity of their love stood as a wall that couldn't be breached.

So, regardless of urgent recommendations from family members to do otherwise, Grandpa nursed and tended to Grandma in the house they'd built together, then when all the hammering was completed, they'd transformed a collection of lumber into a home overcrowded with good memories. In his example of devotion, Grandpa demonstrated the end result and full measure of romance. I think that my grandparents lived the ultimate love story.

After Grandma's funeral, it quickly became apparent that something in my grandfather had died, too. The light in his eyes grew a bit dimmer. His optimism was on a slow, steady decline. Whenever I visited or talked to him on the phone, he'd say, "It'd sure be nice to see you in church on Sunday, Kenny." I'd always respond in a non-committal fashion, but even so, something was changing.

In sorting through sorrow and shame following my grandmother's death, all the stinking garbage piled up inside me shifted to reveal a tender spot that shocked me because of its intensity. It couldn't be denied; I yearned to find my way back to church, if only to encourage or surprise Grandpa.

I was still thrashing around and angry at God, but some deep stirrings within were desperate to reconnect to my spiritual moorings. I didn't actively resist, but a consequence of spitting at grace is that, despite the fact that God continues to offer it, one is deceived into thinking that forgiveness and redemption are only words. I was an exiled man.

Pride had created walls and grand illusions. It'd take five more years before I'd find directions home, and even then, it required the bent wreckage of an automobile.

4

Season of Reconciliation

"Come to me all you who are weary and burdened,
and I will give you rest. Take my yoke upon you
and learn from me, for I am gentle and humble in heart,
and you will find rest for your souls.
For my yoke is easy and my burden is light."

~Jesus of Nazareth~

IN JANUARY 1989 GOD got my attention. It was a perfect mid-winter day, with a blue sky that had no end in sight. The roads were clear and dry, which was good because I was hustling to make a living, driving cab for 4500 Taxi in Welland. It wasn't paying all the bills, but employment-wise, it was what was available to me. It was by far one of the best jobs I ever had. Financially speaking it was a bust, but it was an absolute joy racing around back and side streets in someone else's wheels.

When God rapped on the door of my heart it was as subtle as a baseball bat upside my head, which, given my pigheaded ways, was likely entirely necessary. I was in an accident where the car I was driving skidded down an embankment and rolled over at least three times. At fifty-odd miles per hour, a car cut me off, and I reacted instinctively to avoid it.

It happened fast, but from my perspective there was a crazy slow-motion effect in play. I saw the driver's wide-open eyes and shocked grimace as I swerved past. By all accounts, we should have collided, but instead, I crossed lanes and struck the left-side soft shoulder of the high-way. The tires bit into the gravel, which propelled the vehicle down into the ditch. I tumbled around, smashing into the windshield more than once. No, I wasn't wearing a seatbelt.

When the automobile rocked to a stop, I checked my bearings. There was no blood on the shattered windshield. I quickly looked around the interior. There was no blood splattered on the dashboard or anywhere. For some reason, that fact made a strong impression on me. I felt my face with care, then did a quick inventory to note that all body parts were in place and seemed to be functioning fine.

I grabbed the microphone and reported to the dispatcher. The disembodied voice came back on the two-way radio assuring me that an ambulance was on its way. I started to protest, but then a voice outside the car was calling to me.

A good Samaritan had stopped and was opening the front passenger door. He helped me out. The smell of gasoline seemed to be everywhere, and he hurried me up the steep slope. 4500's fleet was powered by propane, but this particular one was a new acquisition which hadn't yet been modified. It was scheduled to undergo the conversion process the next day, but that was not to be because the car was totaled; a complete write-off.

There was a small crowd gathering at the side of the road. Their faces were all sketched in various expressions of awe, as though they were looking at a walking dead man. The driver who had failed to yield was shaken up, apologizing profusely. I mumbled something. Someone handed me a cigarette, but I couldn't get it lit. My hands were shaking. After several frustrating tries, someone lit it for me. I pulled the smoke deep into my lungs and held it there, staring at the wreck at the bottom of the ditch.

It had come to a rest on its wheels. The roof was partially collapsed, and the front end was twisted. My good fortune didn't escape me. I'd seen other crash sites with much less damage which had resulted in serious injury or death. I released the first drag in a gasp and immediately drew another long one. The palsy in my hands was taking over my whole body. I felt weak and sick to my stomach.

A fellow cabbie arrived while the sirens of the police and/or ambulance were still off in the distance. I dropped into the front seat and told him to take me home. He swore at me. I swore back. Then, with some colorful language, he convinced me to go to the hospital as a precaution. He was persistent. The fear or wonder on his face alarmed me. I shrugged in agreement, then requested that the dispatcher call Anita to let her know that there was nothing wrong with me. I was going to the hospital just to be safe. I replaced the microphone on its hook and hunched up my shoulders. I was sweaty and cold.

"You should be dead," my friend said directly.

I gave him a sideways look. "What?"

"Did you see that car? You should be dead."

"Yeah," I answered. "I should be dead."

Realization was a frigid thing gnawing away at me. After providing preliminary information to the nurse on duty, I was taken down the hall. An extensive series of X-rays were taken, then I was put in an examining room to wait for a doctor.

It turned into a long wait, and being alone gave me time to think and weigh stuff. My life was in shambles. It was a perverse mindset, but I had come to thoroughly believe that a rendezvous with violent death was stalking me. Here I was, on a stretcher instead of a slab in the morgue, but I was so messed up that I actually wondered if I should be relieved that I was alive or bitter because I'd have to keep grinding my life into dust. I carried a deadness around with me while steadily tracking along on a treadmill to nowhere.

Hopes and dreams were nonexistence, buried beneath much self-inflicted misery. The calendar on the wall inserted one more factor into the crazed evaluation churning through my skull. As it happened, it was the day before my father's birthday.

Psychologically, I was terrified; spiritually, I was free- falling. It was a long way to fall. Did I have a death wish; was dying preferable to living? Looking into myself scared me. Every dark emotion was cut loose in a swirling pandemonium that raked me with no remorse. I wanted to flip a switch inside and make it stop.

At the end of me, not knowing what else to do, I groped around and reached out to God. Lying in that sterile cubicle, I prayed. The conversation was faltering, but it was heartfelt. There wasn't much re-ligiously-correct language as I unloaded raw feelings. Utterly aware of my aloneness, I stared at the ceiling and unraveled. Pain, hurt and grief flooded out of me in silent teeth-clenched agony. Questions swirled as memories trickled and flashed in rapid succession.

Waves of grief mixed with waves of guilt. Grief for my father; guilt for how I'd wasted my life and ill-treated those who loved me. My stomach filled with a long-brewed stew of bile as I ranted at God. Where had he been through all the black confusion of my life?

The answer came without warning. There, alone in that hospital emergency room, God made his presence extremely real to me. There were no flashing lights or any high-energy hoopla, but simply a supernatural warmth that settled deep within me. A peace beyond my capacity to comprehend quieted my heart. A powerful sense of belonging and being loved wrapped itself around me, so compelling that it was *almost* physical.

I bent my tear-filled eyes around the room, truly wondering if I was really alone. It came to me that God had always been with me; he had never abandoned me. I had abandoned him; I had chosen to go into the belly of a beast that was chewing me up with a vile glee.

Now there was this flickering glimpse of hope or challenge burning me from the inside out. Whatever it was, I wanted so badly to see it clearly enough to latch onto it. I wanted to put all the mistakes and wrong directions behind me. There were many fences to repair and bridges to be rebuilt, but the opportunity for rescue or deliverance from the beast felt like a tangible possibility.

In the full brightness of that riveting moment, the idea that the foul chaos of my life could be redeemed wasn't a laughing matter. The concept took root. It was fragile, yet forceful. Right there and then I decided to make amends and change my life.

At about this point, the doctor came to tell me that the battery of X-rays were all negative. He did a cursory examination, declared me to be one lucky individual, then released me with written instructions on how to care for the small bump on my forehead and the bruise on my leg. That was the extent of my injuries.

A strange sensation that was foreign to me swelled up within. It took a moment to identify it as gratitude. A smile came, and I knew for a fact that it was no sin or crime to be alive; or to be glad and grateful about being alive. That idea looped itself in my head accompanied by a celebratory melody, which formed a nice grid for me to interpret the last several hours.

There was much to consider as I went home. The accident that'd unleashed all these questions about death and destiny; the tangle of emotions that'd forced me to examine the scarred ruins of my life; the surreal spiritual experience that'd given me a peek at what hope looked like embedded in grace; the determined desire to change my life that'd already become something of a dilemma because I was completely lost as to what steps to take.

Crisis decisions are never easy to follow through on, especially when they occur in a vacuum. I had neither strategy nor plan on how to proceed, and because of my progressive social isolation, I had no one to turn to for advice or counsel.

That evening, after our sons were off to bed, Anita and I talked, and though I may have said a lot, I did not really tell her much at all. I tried to open up and come clean. I wanted to get her insight, but for reasons unknown, I didn't say anything about my prayer, the intensity of the answer, or of my aspiration for atonement and redemption. She even gave me an easy opportunity by raising the issue of us going to church sometime soon. I surely sloughed it off with some witty remark, but the reality was that she'd struck a nerve.

At some deep level I understood that, for me to get right with God, I needed to go back to church. Much more specific than that, I had to return to the church of my childhood.

Once again, even though I had no comprehension of it at the time, the theology of place was active in my life. My mother had carried me to the Sunbeam Sunday School as a newborn baby, and in the back of my mind, I knew that the Port Colborne BIC Church was home. It was where I had grown up, learned about Jesus, made a decision for Christ, and had known God's call to the ministry.

Without any rhyme, reason, or explanation, it was seared into me that, to get right with God, I had to return to that particular church. Whether it was right or wrong thinking is not a debatable matter; it was my mindset, and as everyone knows, mindset has a definite influence on behavior. But how could I go back there?

How could I go back there? The question troubled me. There were far too many broken relationships to ever think that anyone even cared whether I was dead or alive. I believed that lie wholeheartedly, but it was at odds with something else that was having an impact on me. Though I didn't fully possess it, there settled in me a sense of hope which became increasingly difficult to ignore.

Even as the initial warmth of the experience in the hospital room diminished, it had a flashback quality that was intense, and though I kept it to myself, the profound awareness of God was consistently present. I was unable to shake loose from that embrace of everlasting love or hope for redemption. Nor could I delude myself with the view that it was wishful thinking or nothing more than the side effects of shock.

That is not to say that I didn't engage in serious self-delusion. I convinced myself that I had to become good enough for church before I could ever entertain the option of returning. It was just another of the deceiver's great lies that I'd internalized, but in this particular instance, it worked in my favor.

I'm hard-wired with an incessant need to *do something*, so I quietly set about figuring ways to be a better person. There was much to do, and in proceeding, I discovered that there was a whole other person straining to get out from under all the rottenness.

It was plainly in my mind to surprise my grandfather some Sunday morning, and now I had the semblance of a plan. It'd take another year because there would be some false starts and spinning wheels, but at least I was heading in the right direction. Over the next few months, while I toiled on my private self-improvement project, God orchestrated a series of circumstances and contacts that drew me out of myself and edged me ever closer to reconciliation.

In August 1989, after nearly twenty years of an addiction, I successfully quit smoking. It was accomplished cold turkey and appeared to be spontaneous, but had actually been carefully plotted. I had mentally prepared and determined the exact timing.

For two weeks leading up to the last ingestion of nicotine, I worked the graveyard shift dispatching cabs, all the while deliberately indulging myself by chain smoking non-stop. At seven o'clock on the morning of the final shift, I sat and talked with the gathering day-shift drivers, savoring a cigarette and a coffee. When the moment came to pinch the butt into the ashtray, I formally announced that it was my last cigarette. The assembled cabbies laughed, but I insisted.

It was all part of the new and improved version of me. Arriving home that morning, I set about to purposefully carry out my plan. I bleached and scrubbed my fingers to eliminate the yellow stains and stench. When I was satisfied with the results, I proceeded to repeatedly brush my teeth and thoroughly punish my gums before gargling several times. Then I showered and went to bed. Waking up later, I told Anita to throw away whatever tobacco products that might be stashed around the house and to also pack up any and all smoking paraphernalia. She did so with a knowing smile, but no questions.

Over the next several days, I outlasted the physical withdrawal by drinking gallons of black coffee and staying busy. The reality is that the physical addiction was the easy part. It was the emotional or psychological addiction that proved to be the most difficult.

I toughed it out by implementing old-fashioned stubbornness, but the need lingered as a real desire for a long time. In some ways, because of nicotine's insidious nature combined with how original sin infected my makeup and personalized my deepest weaknesses, the emotional or psychological aspects of the addiction likely remains to this day.

There are no cravings or anything like that, but a knowledge abides in me that causes me to suspect that, if a situation was bent or twisted in a certain way, I could light up tomorrow or the next day. How's that for a blast of undiluted honesty?

Earlier that summer, while coaching Little League, I came into contact with a man in the life insurance business. One evening after a game, he proposed that I drop by his office for a preliminary interview with his boss. I thought he was crazy. Given the fact that we were constantly economically challenged, the idea of me being in the financial planning business was bizarrely humorous, but I was intrigued. A meeting was set up, to which I went in a state of apprehension, not knowing what to expect. It went well, and before I realized it, I was busily doing several aptitude tests, all of which I apparently aced.

I saw it as a door opened for me to step through and make some serious gains in self-improvement. Over the course of that summer and autumn, while driving and dispatching cabs, I studied the manuals in preparation for the licensing exam and attended marketing training classes sponsored by the company. The book work and seminars were all interesting, but not at all challenging because I seemed to have an innate disposition for the nuts and bolts of it.

What stretched me the most was coming out of myself. It was an obstacle that frustrated me because I had no frame of reference to comprehend what was happening. The changes in me were worthy, and the necessity to go forward motivated me. I plugged away at it with a workmanlike diligence, taking one step at a time. In doing so, I uncovered strengths and people skills that were atrophied and out of practice.

One of the assignments, which would prove to be providential, was to develop a list of one hundred individuals I knew and rate them as to their potential earning power. At first it appeared to be a simple enough endeavor, but when I sat down to do it, I began to understand the extent of my isolation. It took all the thinking power at my disposal to come up with that list. I stalled out far short of fifty. To complete it, I had to be creative and indulge in guesswork to categorize each person's financial position.

I used every acquaintance and also had to reach back into past church circles, writing down names of those with whom I'd had no contact with for well over a decade.

I honestly didn't understand the purpose of the exercise. I was simply fixated on getting it done and accomplishing all the requirements.

All the studying and preparation yielded good results. I passed the licensing exam with ease. On the first workday of January 1990, wearing an ill-fitting jacket and tie, and feeling like a phony dressed up to fool everyone, I went to an office, sat behind a desk, and waited for the money to start flowing in.

For the first week, I was given a crash course in life insurance products available with this particular company. It was somewhat unreal. At home we were shuffling bills from one pile to another while ranking them as to the most urgent to be paid, and here I was being schooled about tax shelters and maximizing pay-outs. At home we were utilizing whatever loose change we could scrape up to be able to buy milk, and here I was seriously discussing million dollar deals. It's no wonder that within a short time I acquired a low-grade full-time headache.

At the end of that first week I was looking for an exit strategy, but since quit is not in my vocabulary or make-up, I sucked it up and soldiered on. I decided that no matter what it took, I'd succeed because I'd failed in so many other areas of my life. This would be the hill that I'd die on. When the second week started, my manager, a high-energy type-A personality juiced up on ambition, came into my office. We were scheduled to have a prospect development session. I expected him to hand over files of company clients, which he would help me prioritize or give me instructions on how to do business and keep the customers satisfied, but there were no such files for me to glean. What he had for me was a surprise, though looking back I realize that having had no business-world experience, I was under some innocent illusions. He handed me my list of one hundred names and told me to start with it.

"What do you mean?"

"Contact every one of them," he replied nonchalantly.

"For what reason?"

His face wrinkled up in laughter. "To sell them life insurance."

He proceeded to explain how to go about the task. There were addresses and phone numbers to find, an introductory letter to write, then a follow-up plan. When he left me alone, I looked over my list, vaguely wondering if there was some way to avoid doing the job. I felt like I'd been manipulated. I'd developed the list because it was presented as part of the assigned work to get licensed, having no inkling that there would be an expectation for me to do business with any of these people. I quietly cussed myself out for being so stupid, then after exhausting the moment, got down to gathering the necessary information on each name. It took me down more than a few bunny trails, with some unforeseen detours along memory lane. I was especially drawn to those names that were from a whole other lifetime, when I was a different person in a different place.

In the days ahead, I faithfully fulfilled part of the assignment. The letters were prepared, addressed and mailed. It was a matter of time and task management, but the follow-up phone calls would require summoning up the nerve and audacity to put myself on the line, no pun intended. Each time I worked my prospect list, I'd push at it with an enthusiasm couched in frustration.

The phone calls proved to be something of a hit and miss proposition, since I chose not to avail myself of a bit of technology that had become all the rage. I flat-out refused to leave a message for anyone with the simple proclamation: "I don't talk to machines." To me, regardless of the convenience or need, there was something disconnecting and dehumanizing about the casual ease with which we'd accepted the entire concept. I still think that, but even so, I've relented in my inflexibility, and on occasion leave voice mail.

One of the people I'd written a letter to was named Rick. He was a few years younger than I, but there'd been a pleasantly boisterous weekend retreat at Cave Springs Camp that we'd shared. That memory revived when I found his address. He was the son of a couple, who after my father's death, took on the legal task of being my guardians. Mom had been afraid that something would happen to her, so she went through the legal procedure of making sure we'd not be without an anchor.

The second or third time I tried calling Rick, he answered the phone. His voice lit up; he sounded genuinely pleased to hear from me and expressed a desire to get together. An appointment was set, and I hadn't even gotten a chance to use my script.

On a Thursday evening in February, under the canopy of a clear star-speckled sky, I drove out to Wainfleet with the bold and sole intention of presenting my spiel. I was going to move him through the stages to the point of a sale. In this I was to be thwarted because evidently God had some other agenda. Rick met me on the front stoop with a display of the brashness of his personality, which released whatever tension or apprehension there may have been present. Despite the cold, he was wearing shorts and made a comment about how ridiculous it was for me to dress up in a suit to visit an old friend.

After introducing me to his wife, we settled in the living room and immediately began to reminisce. It quickly became apparent that all our stories were intertwined with church activities and tied to faith journey milestones. Time became a fast train racing through the night with no regard for anything except the rites of restoration along the track toward reconciliation. One tale naturally gave way to another as we regaled each other, embellishing here and there as laughter filled the room.

The free flow of humor put into motion a wall collapsing process that provided a way for us to creep closer to matters of the heart, and finally we began touching on hardships and difficulties. His experience as an adult was checkered with struggles to which I could easily identify. His disillusionments were different, but there was a sameness to them that sparked empathy in me.

I listened, all the while aware of warmth surfacing within me. He spoke boldly about grace, which stirred the embers of hope I had into a tiny flame. He'd recently found his way back into church life, and now he talked animatedly about the church, its new pastor, and my grandfather. He'd obviously established a strong relationship with Grandpa, which was encouraging.

Many hours had passed when he told me that I needed to get myself back to church. I shot back a well-practiced song and dance which consisted of lame excuses as to why that'd be impossible, but even I could hear that there was no conviction in my voice. He pressed, unwilling to hear a negative answer. I departed some time after midnight, assuring him that I'd at least call the pastor and talk to him.

The next morning, with the door firmly closed, I sat in my life insurance office, holding the phone's receiver while staring at the keypad as though it was too hot to handle. I don't recall how long it took to convince myself to do the deed, but I can say that it was an elasticized stretch of time.

Eventually I punched out the seven digits, took a deep breath and seriously wished for it to ring off the hook. It didn't. A male voice answered, and I asked to speak to the pastor. He said that he was the pastor. His name was Brian. I introduced myself, and a cheer-filled chuckle filled my ear. I frowned and ignored it.

"You don't know me, but . . ."

"I've heard lots about you. You're Percy's grandson."

"Yeah. Listen. You got time for a coffee or something?"

"Sure. Name where and when."

I paused. The silence became uncomfortable and I wanted to hang up. He broke the moment, "Sometime this afternoon? Tim Hortons?"

"No," I answered, resolve stiffening in me. "What about tomorrow morning? At the church? I'd like to see the place again."

"Okay. Does nine o'clock work?"

"Yeah."

"See you then."

I hung up without saying anything else. It was strange. There were so many wildly diverse emotions running loose inside me. I tried concentrating on work, but it was fruitless. I couldn't shut down or even slow the past as it rolled through my head. I replayed many details about my faith experience with a mixture of wonder and fear. Could my life be redeemed?

I left the office under the pretense that I'd be out and about prospecting, but in reality, all thoughts regarding the life insurance business were so far away as to be non-existent. Paying homage to Shakespeare's *Macbeth*, I was busily *screwing my courage to the sticking post*, mentally preparing to go back to a gray-stone building that'd been the place of my spiritual awakening and development.

I drove around aimlessly several hours, reworking bygone days over and over, arriving at a singular conclusion: I couldn't change nor fix the past; I couldn't even put a sugary glaze on my life.

The sun had crossed its apex when I parked beside the Welland Canal and stared at its snow blanketed surface while making a long sojourn through the dark valleys on the landscape of memory. It was February. Though it was a bright winter day, I conjured up a faraway February and the frozen wasteland of Lake Erie on the evening of the day my father had been killed.

It came rushing back with a vibrancy that made the years disappear. All of a sudden I was seemingly watching the fifteen-year- old version of myself. I heard the anguished cry questioning God: "Why?" I let its echo momentarily bounce around my skull, then firmly silenced it. There was no reason to listen to it because there'd be no answer forthcoming that would satisfy the pain or human reasoning.

Bad stuff happens in life. It's that simple. I'd resigned myself to the fact that God wasn't required to explain himself to me. And even if he'd provide an explanation, my brain was too feeble to comprehend.

Brooding on an endless sequence of considerations about God and hope and destiny, I went home early, before our sons were out of school. Anita and I talked everything over, then I circled to come at it from another angle, raising objections and protests, which were dismantled one by one. She was so supportive, she made me mad.

I was seeking someone who would let me off the hook or talk me out of meeting with the pastor, and all she did was listen to my ramblings while gently prodding me to stand up and be a man. She would never say those words or anything even remotely close to them, but that's what I heard in her quiet voice and saw in the intense blue of her pretty eyes.

Saturday morning, driving to the church, I actually prayed. I don't recollect the words or any request, but I suspect it'd have something to do with standing up and being a man. A wave of emotion crashed up against me when I pulled into the parking lot, so much so that I felt tears fill my eyes. I fought them back, sat in the car until I had all my feelings knotted down, and then went into the building.

Brian was at the top of the stairs to greet me with a friendly smile and booming welcome that was authentic. I'd always had a sensitive antenna for phoniness, and my short exposure to the ways of the life insurance business had increased that awareness.

There was nothing fake or bogus in the man who gave me a firm handshake. We sat in his office and jumped right into it. He didn't ask any questions, but began by telling me about himself. We connected, but since it'd been so long since I'd been open with anyone, I didn't even identify what was happening.

There were some similarities in our stories. He'd hit a couple rough patches in life, and there'd even been a time when God had gotten his attention in the midst of tragedy. He and his wife's first child, a son named Jason, died several hours after being born. His voice grew thick as he shared this, and God used his naked honesty about such a painful memory to soften me.

I also remember being impressed, that between stints in Bible College, he'd worked as a roofer. As it turned out his practically applied theology would always appeal to my blue-collar sensibilities.

After an hour or so, we toured the facility, which brought back so many good memories that I couldn't grasp them as they swirled through my brain. We chatted about me returning to church and what that would look like.

Brian told me two things that have always stuck with me: My family and I would be warmly welcomed and accepted, and taking that first step would be the one that'd make all the difference. He said that the longer it took to follow-through on my intention to come back to church, the more difficult it would become.

I warned him that if and when I showed up, it wouldn't be as a bystander on the fringe of things, but that I'd be in for a penny, in for a pound. He let out a loud gust of laughter and said that'd be just fine. Before leaving, in some way that I never saw coming, he extracted a promise from me that I would have my family in church the next morning.

Heading home, I felt a little giddy with a strong undercurrent of an unknown emotion percolating, which I managed to determine was relief. I took a roundabout route, continuing the process of preparation, running through various scenarios of the next day. When I arrived at the house, Anita could see something in my smile that caused the twinkle in her eyes to flash with a brightness that disarmed me. Before I had my coat off, I asked what she thought about us going back to church.

"When?"

"Tomorrow."

"It's about time," she said, giving me a hug. We held each other for long time, and all the while I kept my tear ducts dammed up, though a few trickled out. We called our sons together for a family meeting to tell them. Their response was a collective shrug along with a few questions about why we were making such a big deal about it. Church wasn't new to them. At Anita's insistence, and to ease my conscience, we had been sending them to a church that had a bus ministry, but the new emphasis of us going along with them to a different church was a dynamic that appeared to puzzle them.

On the morning of February 11, 1990 I emerged from my self-imposed exile and returned to the Port Colborne Church with my wife and four sons. I remember the date exactly because, in an ironic twist that never occurred to me until years later, it was the day Nelson Mandela was released from prison in South Africa. His prison of concrete and barbed wire had been forged by political and racial oppression, whereas my self-created dungeon tower had been built with the bricks of delayed grief held together by the mortar of stubbornness, stupidity, and pride.

As a charter member and elder statesman of the congregation, Grandpa Major had assumed the role of official greeter. When we entered the foyer and my eyes met his, the surprised expression on his face momentarily betrayed his joy, but being stoic by both nature and nurture, he quickly recovered. Even so, the false front was flimsy because his rejoicing was evident, as was the moisture glistening behind his glasses. With the formality of his British heritage, accompanied by that habitual click-click sound he made with his mouth, he introduced us to whoever walked past. There were several impromptu reunions. Received with open arms and warm words, we made our way into the sanctuary and found a pew.

Feelings can be a puzzle, and one ought to never base their perspective on them, but as I sat there, it came to me that the place *felt* the same; in fact, it *felt* good. There was something comforting in the sameness of the windows, the lighting, and the heavy beams in the ceiling.

The service began with the worship leader, a gregarious man who had known me all my life, referencing current events in the context of being thankful for God's faithfulness. He noted the celebration on the news that morning, with scenes from South Africa of little children dancing because of Mandela's release.

I made it through the opening hymns, Scripture reading, and prayer time with my emotions tethered on a short leash. Then according to the bulletin, just before the message, a men's trio was to provide special music.

I watched with interest as they took their place behind the pulpit because, in my previous life, I had known all three of them: Merle, Blain, and Rick. I watched them, being careful to remain disengaged, but that was destined to be a futile exercise. God was about to grab my heart and give it a definitive squeeze that'd transform me into a shivering hulk of a man. All the hateful words I'd freely hurled at God were about to be gathered in a tumultuous deluge of his sovereignty.

Every pain-racked excess of guilt had an appointment with an outrageous grace that'd shatter my resistance to his forgiveness and love. I had labored hard to secure my prison, but in an instant, God smashed the walls down with the profound simplicity of a song.

Three notes in on the piano, and as the old game show bit goes, I could name that tune, and was startled by the sheer force of that recognition. I winced because I'd bitten my bottom lip hard enough to taste blood as the harmonized words filled the sanctuary and swelled inside me:

> *"O Lord my God, when I in awesome wonder,*
> *Consider all the worlds thy hands have made,*
> *I see the stars, I hear the rolling thunder,*
> *Thy power throughout the universe displayed.*
> *Then sings my soul, my Savior God, to thee;*
> *How great thou art, how great thou art!*
> *Then sings my soul, my Savior God, to thee;*
> *How great thou art, how great thou art!"*

Halfway through the first verse, tears started. It was a trickle that I tried to contain, but soon my cheeks were soaked as my tightly wrapped emotions came completely undone. Pride tried with all it was worth to stomp down the remorse, but it poured out of me. Cognizant of the sideways glances of our sons, I struggled to maintain composure, but it was a losing battle. I hung my head and wept.

My mind raced backwards through the years and across the miles. It settled on a springtime evening before life happened and I lost my way, when a red-faced preacher had rhythmically cried out, "My God, my God, how great thou art!"

The impossibility of coincidence wrecked me. It was too much to reason away or slough off. Of all the possible song choices, how could those three men have selected *How Great Thou Art* for special music? In choosing that song, none of them could have been sure of who'd be there that morning or how God was at work in their midst. It was inconceivable.

Even if they'd known I'd be there, they had no knowledge about the benchmark nature of that song in my life. I was experiencing an inner meltdown that required all the self-control I possessed to reign in my emotions. I didn't listen to a word of the sermon because my mind was too busy attempting to comprehend the far-reaching ramifications of this incredible demonstration of God's sovereignty. The impossibility of it defied coincidence.

When the service closed, I wanted nothing more than to escape. Red-eyed and somewhat ashamed, I kept my family herded together and hurried them out of the building. People were friendly, but I hustled past them and assiduously avoided eye contact, trying to keep chit-chat to a minimum.

Of course, Brian, being the epitome of a pastor was positioned near the exit. He shook our hands, having something positive to say to each one.

Outside, the air was cold, with the sky a crisp blue that promised warmer days ahead. While we waited for a few moments for the defrost to kick in, our oldest son, soon to be fifteen years old, tentatively voiced what his brothers must have been thinking.

"Are you okay, Dad?"

The worry in his tone touched me. "Yeah," I grunted. "I'll be fine."

Anita turned toward the back seat and asked, "How did you boys like that?"

There was a flurry of answers, with the consensus being that it was good; not a negative report from any of them. Their only question: "Are we going back?"

"Yes," Anita said decisively. "In fact, later today."

"What?" I asked, frowning at her.

"Choir practice for Easter starts this afternoon. And I want to sing in it," she said, showing me the announcement in the bulletin. Resignation did a slow twist in me, and I gave her a nod in agreement. There'd be no discussion because I knew her tone and resolve well. I also remembered my words about being in for a penny, in for a pound, so that, as they say, was that. Case closed.

Over the next several months, we were intentional about integrating church into our lives. It wasn't as hard as I'd imagined. Anita and our sons jumped right into activities and started making new friends, which was somehow rewarding for me to watch. In it I saw a glimpse of God's goodness, which made me want to get hold of it for myself, but there remained an entrenched resistance. For the first couple weeks, I attempted to merely go through the motions, doing my best to keep God at arm's length, but he had other plans and was wasting no time or effort. He was at work in ways that had to be acknowledged.

For me, freely accepting the grace offered by God and the friendship of others had its difficult aspects. There was too much junk buried in the debris of the shattered prison walls. I began to sort through it all, and as I did so, I made a temporary truce with God. It wasn't the kind of peace settlement that comes with unconditional surrender, but rather, it had provisional elements. All I did was crack open the door of my heart, but God used that small act to create space for me to work through accumulated garbage in the context of a faith community.

It was a hesitant beginning, but I made an effort to read my Bible for purely devotional reasons. Mostly I felt like an imposter inside of someone else's skin. It seemed as though I was being watched over my shoulder whenever I blocked out quiet time, but I kept at it. I deliberately began with the book of John. Rather than being drenched in doubt and looking for loop-holes or reasons for an argument, I just read it.

It wasn't long before what I'd known about the Bible since childhood became real to me again. It was God's Word, plain and simple. And surprise of surprises, God's Word began to do in me what God's Word does. It changed me; it caused me to consider life from its perspective.

The stinky fertilizer of grief had rich nutrients that had seeped into my soul, and now it started to produce rapid spiritual growth. Quite frankly, it was an amazing process to experience. All the Bible stories I'd learned as a child took on multi-dimensional meaning that spoke truth to my life.

As my relationship with God was restored and renewed, I started to open up to others and allowed the body of Christ and God's love to touch me deeply. Brian and I met each week for a Bible study, which was truly enriching. Exploring Scripture together was good, but it was the friendship that God used to draw me out of my myopia.

Even so, with God obviously at work, from that first morning back at church, there was something within that was quietly unsettled. I couldn't put my finger on what was ill at ease, but there was definitely something going on in my heart.

Someone directed me to the book of Lamentations. It was just an off-hand remark during a discussion, but as it turned out, Jeremiah, the weeping prophet, had something incredible to teach me. Over the course of months, verses nineteen thru twenty-four of the third chapter became a daily mantra for me:

"I remember my affliction and my wandering, the bitterness and the gall. I well remember them, and my soul is downcast within me. Yet this I call to mind and therefore I have hope: Because of the LORD's great love we are not consumed, for his compassions never fail. They are new every morning; great is your faithfulness. I say to myself, 'The LORD is my portion; therefore I will wait for him.'"

In August 1990, I would discover exactly what the undercurrent of unease was all about. It would come blazing at me to change the course of my life completely. The setting was Niagara Campmeeting, an annual week-long gathering alongside the Niagara River on the campus of what was then known as Niagara Christian College. It had been an important venue of my childhood and early teen years, but I hadn't attended since 1974, so there were many reconnections to be made.

At an evening session early in the week, Anita and I were standing beside each other singing along with the assembled crowd. We'd arrived late, so we were near the back of the large auditorium. The song was *Great Is Thy Faithfulness*. When we completed the first verse and started on the chorus, a small voice as clear as clear can be spoke in my mind: *Yes, I have been faithful. Where have you been?*

It was not audible, but it was so close to being audible that I actually looked around to see if there was someone there or if anyone else had heard it. Its echo rippled through me and in its wake an instantaneous understanding. My mouth dried up. There could be no denying or pretending about the meaning of those words: *Yes, I have been faithful. Where have you been?*

I knew that God was speaking to me about the call to pastoral ministry. It had been tossed aside and nearly drowned in alcohol, but here it was, resurfacing to demand an answer. All at once, I got the cold sweats and hot flashes, which was weird in the extreme. My legs felt weak and unsteady, and my eyes were watery. I dropped my corner of the hymnal as though it had burned me and sat down.

Anita shot me a questioning look. I ignored her and everything else as an interior tension worked me over. It was adamant and wouldn't be silenced, seemingly wanting it all settled right there and then, but being the personification of stubbornness, that wasn't about to happen. The whole idea was preposterous. I was too old, and there'd been too many miles running down back streets.

My protestations were loud in my mind, but were gaining no traction. While the rest of the service unfolded, there was no comfort or relief for me.

I have no idea what the preacher's text or sermon was about that evening. I didn't hear a single word of it. He could have recited Dr. Suess or read the telephone book, and God would have used it to captivate my attention. Apparently there are moments when God makes himself heard.

Later, when we were alone in the car driving home, Anita waited a fair amount of time for me to say something, but when I didn't, she initiated conversation with a direct question.

"What was that all about?"

"I don't know."

"Yes, you do," she insisted.

I paused to form my words carefully. It was a long moment, and I could sense her eyes on me. "It's too crazy to be real, but I think God wants me to build an ark," I said, trying to diminish the enormity of it with humor.

"Oh, I see," she replied sharply. "Why don't you tell me the truth?"

"I'm scared," I admitted with a helpless shrug. Then, after a slow release of air, I proceeded to tell her as best I could what had occurred. She listened as I spoke in measured tones. Saying it aloud didn't make it sound any less ridiculous to me. When I came to a natural break, she allowed perhaps a full five seconds to pass before her words confronted the obvious.

"What are you going to do?"

"Find a place to hide."

"No," she said, "you've already done too much of that."

"Yeah, well . . ."

"Yeah, well nothing," she cut me off with a determination that slapped at me.

"What am I supposed to do?" I shot back, glancing at her.

"Pray," she replied softly. "I'll pray for you."

How was I supposed to respond to that? She was being so reasonable about it, and I was convicted and impressed by her effortless expression of faith. It wasn't a new experience for me. I wanted to pull her close and push her away all at the same time, which was also not a new experience. A moment passed in which I made allowance that prayer could be an option; perhaps the only option. I reached out, held her hand, and said thank you by giving it a gentle squeeze.

For the next month, we kept the incident to ourselves. It was our secret, so much so that we hardly mentioned it. There was no reason to because its presence was made known in all the unspoken words. Whenever bravery would rise in me, I'd broach the topic with her. She'd listen and carefully offer encouragement, but she never once initiated dialogue on the issue. She respected the privacy of it and gave me room. Her attitude could infuriate me because she had this assurance that everything would work itself out, but regardless of how many times I turned it over to figure the angles, I couldn't. It didn't make any sense.

I wrestled with God, cantankerously refusing him. Years of practice had me fully acquainted with the fierce ins and outs of this sort of grappling. I was willing to do anything rather than be pinned down and give an affirmative answer to the call to pastoral ministry. There was no way that was going to happen. All the tumblers weren't going to click into place because the door to that possibility had been hammered shut with an over-abundance of nails. I had screwed my life up too royally for that to even be put into consideration.

God couldn't be serious; he simply had to be mistaken on this one, but he wouldn't leave me alone. I was unable to shake free of his grasp. The words were always at the edge of everything, their meaning constantly clear: *Yes, I have been faithful. Where have you been?*

With my attention riveted on coming to terms with those words, there were many late night negotiation sessions in which I'd try to cut a deal with God. In all earnestness, I offered everything I could dream up, but nothing placated him or caused the words to fade into the background noise of life. I thought I was being entirely fair and honest in bargaining a compromise, but evidently, when God calls, there's only one acceptable answer, and he goes deaf until he hears it.

After stringing together numerous sleepless nights, with the angst becoming increasingly desperate, I wanted relief or release or something. One mid-September evening, without any prompting from Anita, I invited myself over to the parsonage for a meeting with Pastor Brian and Liz. They were gracious.

The discussion began with me prefacing everything in the unknown and referencing the lame remark about building an ark, which elicited a hearty laugh from Brian, but his demeanor soon changed. As I got down to the nitty gritty, he grew intensely serious and was all business. He listened with a small smile, as though he already knew the story and was aware of my ongoing inner turmoil. He asked a pertinent question here and there, but mostly he just nodded.

It all came rushing out of me. I didn't hold anything back, then concluded with the question, "What do I do now?"

"That's great!" Brian exclaimed excitedly.

"What's great about it, Brian? I think I'm losing my mind."

"It's great that you're wrestling with God," he replied in a firm voice. "God wants to do something in you, and you're listening to him. That's great."

"So why doesn't it feel great?"

"You're looking too far down the road," he answered, shifting forward. "You got all these questions, but all you need to do is take one step at a time."

Liz agreed. "When we came to ministry, it was a whole bunch of little steps."

I frowned hard at her. "What's my first step?"

"It'd be the next step," she replied pointedly.

"That's right," Brian said, chuckling. "You've already taken a first step."

"Okay. What's the next step?" I wondered, sounding frustrated.

"Test the call," he said quickly. "A practical way to do that is to get involved in ministry right here and see if there's any affirmation from God or others."

The conversation continued for quite awhile. We talked about how our sons would react to this step, recognizing that their support would be necessary. We considered my gift-mix, and there was general consensus about which areas of ministry would be best suited for me. We even got specific, all of which I greeted with a curious mix of hesitancy and boldness.

I was told that Anita would be an essential element and crucial asset in ministry. I instinctively knew that, but didn't understand completely at the time. In the ensuing years, it's a truth that I've come to fully appreciate.

Before leaving, we prayed together, and it felt good. A sense of peace blanketed me. Driving home, I was convinced that I'd sincerely answered the call; I thought it was a done deal. I slept soundly that night, waking up refreshed and invigorated, prepared to take hold of whatever ministry opportunity was offered. All those feelings would shortly be a memory.

There were to be a whole slew of sleepless nights in the not too distant future. My insomnia would be tied to the deafness God acquires, which can only be alleviated by the sound of unconditional surrender.

Some of the ideas we talked about that evening got implemented rather quickly. It seemed that, before I knew it, I was leading a small group and teaching a Sunday School class, and both were rewarding. It was all interesting, flexing and growing ministry muscles, but there remained a worrisome restlessness within me. I poured myself into my assignments, faithfully working at it and likely learning more than I was able to teach or facilitate, but no matter what I did, the sense of peace was fleeting and fragile.

By the end of the year it disappeared completely and sleep deprivation became routine. I'd wake up at one or two in the morning and be wide awake for the rest of the night, staring into the darkness and struggling with the insistence of that still small voice: *Yes, I have been faithful. Where have you been?*

Call me crazy, but in the midst of all this, what's clear in hindsight was murky at best. I didn't see that God required blank-check obedience. Perhaps I was obtuse or obstinate; perhaps I simply refused to make that observation; perhaps all the years of hostility had made me susceptible to accepting a certain estrangement in my relationship with God.

Or perhaps it was all necessary in the process of smelting and refining me. I don't know for sure. Maybe it's all of the above, because throughout the give and take tension of wrestling with God, which was accompanied by an absence of peace, I experienced accelerated spiritual growth.

In February 1991, a year after emerging from exile, I was tired and tip-toeing along on an emotional tightrope. The factors for this were many. Living the life I'd lived had produced difficult consequences that couldn't be easily fixed or restored, and some of those were rabidly nipping at my heels.

Yes, God's grace was real and perceptible in my life, but some self-inflicted wounds create troubles and relational chaos requiring years of work to redeem. Yes, God's forgiveness is freedom, and he's always in the business of forgiveness, but some seeds planted grow ugly weeds with deep roots, and some mistakes result in bills of fare we never stop paying for this side of eternity. I was beginning to realize how badly my messed up choices in the past were influencing my present and would impact my future.

Mix into that the whole burden of the call that God wouldn't release me from regardless of how much I dickered with him, and I was in a sorry state of mind. Prompted by the Holy Spirit, I identified an issue in my life that I was unwilling to entrust to God. It was profoundly personal, and I wasn't sure what to do or how to proceed, but now I had some level of comprehension as to why peace was such a rare commodity for me.

At church we embarked on a *Forty Day Spiritual Adventure*. It was a daily devotional during Lent in preparation for Easter. In response to one of its practical application exercises I penned the following poem:

Dull-edged February Thoughts

Junkyard sorrows roam free
while black dogs howl in the rain
and I search the rubble to find me
stuck inside the breakdown lane
used up and running past empty
a china heart shattered by pain
waltzing with the lonely old shadows
turn around, my dear, turn around again.

~

Accusations fly like bullets spark
words of rage hurled at the sky
a blinded warrior lost in the dark
deceived by the tempter's endless lie
but holy love arrows to the mark
to pierce the deathgrip with a loud outcry
and release me from the eternal gallows
turn loose my soul, no more to die.

It didn't occur to me when I wrote it, but at some point along the road of my journey, I realized that this poem actually parallels the passage from Lamentations that was an ongoing lesson for me. Jeremiah had ploughed deep furrows in my psyche, and like a johnny-come-lately discovering it, I had internalized the timeless message. Hope had nothing to do with the circumstances of my life. Genuine hope rested securely in the unchangeable character of God. Real hope had to do with my willingness to trust God in the darkness.

In the poem, I remember the sorrow and afflictions of my life. I remember the pain and loneliness that turned into bitterness and gall. As bleak as all that may be, I recall that holy love broke through all the rubbish to embrace me. Day by day by day, I was being reminded that God's faithfulness to me was fresh each and every morning.

As I continued my knock-down drag-out with God, it settled into me that it was all coming to a head of some kind because the life God allows me is precious to him. And he wasn't finished with me yet. He hadn't brought me out of the belly of the beast and back into his grace to leave me stewing in disobedience. *All of life is preparation and God was working everything together for his purposes.*

As winter gave way to spring, I was being worn down by the spiritual slugfest. I had punched myself out and was staggering to stand, sometimes wondering if I was even still on my feet.

On a Sunday morning in April, there was special music at church. The singer's name was Linda, and she opened the service with a story leading into a song. The story was about Moses standing in front of the burning bush. Referring to his shepherd's staff, God asked him, "What's that in your hand?" She spoke about the stuff we hold in our hands and refuse to release into God's care.

The admonition couldn't be lost on anyone. Whatever we have in our hands must be laid down and released to God for him to use as he sees fit. Just before she began singing, she looked out across the congregation and with a gentle urgency that cut me, she asked, "What's that in your hand?"

As she sang, God crushed me. No one else could possibly know, but I was perfectly aware of what was in my hand. I understood exactly what I was holding back from God because it was in both hands, with my fists clenched around it so tightly that it hurt. Even so, until that soul-defining moment, I would only vaguely admit to myself what I refused to entrust to him.

It was the creative part of me that I'd discovered in the aftermath of sorrow when my friend Queenie died. It was my writing, the balance beam on which my sanity depended. God could have everything else, but I would cling to my writing. It was private; it was *mine*. I had never made a dime with it, but I harbored grand illusions of producing a string of bestselling novels. I wouldn't let go because I'd been deluded into believing that I had to protect it. God would take it away from me, and it'd be gone. I would never be able to daydream in story or rhyme again.

That's one of the deceptions that'd ensnared me for so long, but now, in the sanctuary where the Jesus' vaccination had been administered, all the close quarters combat and infighting with God came to a climax. Every word of the song seemed to be directed at me. I started crying and couldn't contain it.

I suppose it's fair to put it that way because it began as crying, but it was soon much more than merely crying. I was sobbing and couldn't stop. Great heaving sobs ripped out of me. My body hunched over and my shoulders quaked.

The force of my emotions was a swelling wave that wouldn't crest. I was in tears or near tears for the rest of the service. It's a complete blur until the moment Pastor Brian stood to preach. His message was simple, and it went like this:

"I have my sermon notes here," he said, holding them up for all to see. "But God is doing something in some people's lives, and I'm going to get out of the way. If you need to come to the altar and do business with God . . ."

Like the smooth stone that struck Goliath, I shot up out of the pew and couldn't get to the front fast enough. I collapsed on my knees and prayed in submission. Devoid of religious niceties, it roiled up from the deepest well in me.

"I don't care anymore, God. I ain't fighting anymore, and I ain't holding nothing back. Whatever I have to do, I'll do. Wherever you want me to go, I'll go. Whatever hoops I gotta jump through, I'll jump through."

The words came out in guttural slurs, followed by an incredible release. Every bit of resistance was gone. I felt lightheaded and relaxed. I didn't know what it all meant or what God would do with it, but I knew that there was no going back; there was no negotiating left to do.

This wasn't appeasement, for I dictated no terms; this was unconditional surrender, a prayer that'd affect me for the rest of my mortal life. The words never go away, sometimes haunting me and sometimes tempering me. In times of difficulty or when standing at a crossroads, they rush back as a reminder that obedience is a never-ending requirement.

There were others at the altar that day, but I couldn't tell you who or what God was doing in their lives. All I knew was that I'd settled a long-standing issue, but without action, my prayer would be meaningless. Decisions made in full crisis-mode in church on a Sunday morning must be developed into a plan to go forward on Monday. Otherwise, it's all trivial nonsense and chasing the wind.

Shortly after nine the next morning, I called Brian and we talked about it all. He was extremely supportive and told me some steps to take. The fact that he took it all seriously convinced me that I wasn't losing my marbles.

Brian suggested that I call the bishop of the Canadian Conference, and talk it over with him. He gave me the number, and as soon as I hung up with him, I dialed it.

Bishop Dale was a nice man whom I had briefly known for six months or so after I'd dropped out of Bible College. He was a pastor back then and was one of several people who'd reached out to me in an attempt to divert me off the path of self-destruction, but I was too proud and self-absorbed. He wasn't in the office when I called, so I left a message, providing the insurance office number and also my home phone.

The day passed with me tinkering around with administrative paperwork. It was make-work projects, which allowed me to mentally check out. I was consumed with what was going on in my heart. Ideas flickered through my mind as I tried to determine what possible measures could be taken to honor God. It didn't look hopeful to me.

I was thirty-five years old, deeply flawed, and covered with scars. I had family responsibilities. Financially speaking, I was perpetually stuck in the mud. I had nothing to offer except willingness combined with a bull-dog determination to do whatever was necessary to remain true to the intent of the words I'd prayed. Try as I might, I couldn't imagine a realistic plan for that to be accomplished.

Shortly after arriving home, around five-thirty, the phone rang, and it was the bishop. "Hey, Ken. I understand you want to talk to me. What's up?"

"This is going to sound bonkers, and I don't know what it means." I paused, thinking about how to verbalize it, and decided to trot out a lame joke that should have been shot and put out of its misery. "I think God wants me to build an ark."

Dale didn't laugh. Not even a tiny chuckle. Instead he was firm, "God's not asking you to build an ark. God wants you in pastoral ministry."

I swallowed hard, feeling chastised. "Yeah. Is that crazy?"

"Crazy?" Now he laughed easily. "No. If you can be happy doing something else, do it. On many days ministry will drive you crazy, but if God is calling you to it, you'll never be at peace doing anything else," he said.

"So what do I do?"

He told me about some others he'd worked with who'd come to ministry out of different careers. He said he'd use their established pattern as a blueprint, then sketched out a bare-bones plan that'd take on detail in the next number of weeks.

I listened in amazement because he spoke in matter-of-fact terms, giving tremendous credence to my call, which affirmed and fortified me. Each step of the proposed plan was sensible, and by the time I got off the phone, I was excited big-time because it was all do-able: A personal study program sponsored by the denomination based on the principles of TEE (Theological Education by Extension). An internship would be arranged in consultation with the leadership of the Port Colborne Church. After I had more hands-on experience and some course work finished, I'd pursue writing the doctrinal exam.

I immediately jumped in with both feet. In doing so, I likely gave my friend and mentor Brian a few extra gray hairs as I kept at him, asking endless questions and pressing on up a steep learning curve.

One month after I waved the white flag of surrender, God gave me a glimpse of his goodness and provided affirmation that was tailor-made for me. He opened a door for ministry that still boggles my mind, because it was as though God was blessing me for finally responding in a way that honored him.

My first venture into ministry was hanging out with professional baseball players and sitting four rows up on the third base side for every home game. Through a series of circumstances that could only have been arranged by our Heavenly Father, I received a phone call on the Sunday afternoon of Mother's Day. It was from the Minor League Director of Baseball Chapel. He introduced himself, gave me some preliminary information, then asked if I would be willing to serve as chaplain for the Welland Pirates, a Single A affiliate of the Pittsburgh Pirates.

It was a volunteer position, but I didn't hesitate because I'd decided that, since I'd wasted so much of my life, I was going to seize every opportunity God presented. I may have asked one or two questions before responding in the affirmative.

That spring and summer, while continuing to stretch every dollar to make financial ends meet, I had eye-opening experiences in ministry. It was an immersion in people skills development that was almost like learning to swim by getting tossed overboard in the middle of the ocean. I possessed a ton of desire and the outward appearance of self-confidence, and that's about all.

The job stretched me, providing important insights about myself and the meaning of ministry. I pretended I knew what I was doing, but mostly I acted on instinct and made it up as I went along. Time has proven to me that it was a brilliant strategy because, more often than not, instinct and an ability to adapt are essential in working as a shepherd.

I discovered that I had a natural ease in connecting with Latino players. I didn't think of it in these terms, but I was engaged in cross-cultural ministry. It was thrilling, and I unearthed a tenderness in me that had been obscured beneath hard layers of callous.

Despite my mental block or tin ear when it comes to foreign languages, I managed to communicate just fine. After returning from an away game or road trips, there'd be midnight runs to the supermarket for them to stock up on groceries or to look for a restaurant that was still open. They introduced me to Mexican cuisine, which set me off on a continuing quest to find the perfect taco salad.

Talking baseball and getting up-close points about fastballs or cut-sliders from pitchers, or listening to real hitters discuss the varied techniques of hitting was an education beyond my boyhood dreams. In almost every discussion, I sought to intentionally tie in a spiritual or life application point, all of which generated in me a childlike giddiness.

As a life-long baseball fan who used to run home from school during the World Series to keep score with his grandfather, it was almost too good to believe. By the end of the season, I'd decided that I wanted the following chiseled on my tombstone: *All things considered, I'd rather be planted in a ball park.*

In August, with the endorsement of the Port Colborne Church Board, I began an internship under Brian's direction. This wasn't an automatic, nor should it be seen as an inconsequential rubber stamp; this was a huge step taken by people who recognized the uncertainty involved.

After all, they were taking a risk on me and in a way were assuming responsibility for a portion of my training. The Church Board weighed out many factors, then gave unanimous confirmation. For not the first nor last time I had reason to be grateful for the DNA of that church. The overarching principle is about loving and helping people, which had been woven into its genetic code by men and women of faith like George A. Sider and Viola Fretz.

I'll forever be indebted to the lay leadership team that was in place to consider the internship proposal because they had inherited that people-centric DNA. Their vision to break new ground to accommodate me should never be regarded lightly.

God used the personalized internship program to do some things in me that needed doing. It gave me a place to stand. It immersed me in real-life ministry and made allowances for rookie mistakes and misdirected passion. The laboratory of a healthy church in the throes of growth spurts was a remarkable classroom to learn lessons which are still being applied.

Whatever seeds I've been able to plant in the ensuing years were germinated in that cell of the body of Christ because it blessed me with approval and affirmation. Through the grapevine I heard that, after some significant discussion as to details, one member summed up the Church Board's decision with words that went something like this: "If we don't do this, we should get out of the church business."

My first assignment was to preach on a Sunday morning. The idea was a natural, but it set off an anxiety in me that was difficult to subdue. I prayed, studied and considered different passages. After settling on one, I decided to avail myself of a tremendous resource for part of my preparation.

I spent chunks of time talking to Grandpa and picking his brain. He'd listen to my ideas, offer some insights, but mostly he told me to relax and enjoy myself. It was during this time that he gave me the best advice concerning homiletics. Homiletics is the study or theology of the craft of preaching. I've known people who have much more schooling and book learning on the topic than I do. I never made it to a homiletics class because I'd had my coffee and donut at Ontario Bible College before it was on the schedule.

However, no one has ever received more prudent wisdom than what my grandfather offered. When it's implemented, it fills in the blanks with eloquent practicality. Grandpa looked me in the eye and sternly said, "Say what you feel, feel what you say, and never let anyone but God tell you what to say."

By September I was tackling the denomination's personal study program with tenacious boldness. I had also picked up steady pulpit supply work, serving the United Church in two rural communities, Tintern and Silverdale. I was out of life insurance and into life assurance. Apparently the whole gig as a seller of financial products was merely a stepping stone God had placed in my path to get me going in the direction he had planned for me.

I was back driving and dispatching cabs and having lots of fun. The income was still lousy and the hours long, but there was a freedom and flexibility which allowed for lots of study time. Life was full of busyness, and I found I had a latent ability to keep lots of plates spinning at the same time.

During this interval I stumbled upon an idea that has proven to be important. I read an article about developing little observances which would act as a reminder of some aspect of God's character.

These could be anything occurring in the natural world and were referred to as triggers. I meditated on the concept for a long while, then came up with a response that was accidentally brilliant because it tapped into an ingrained interest. To understand the genius of it, I must tell you that, in our family, bird watching is a generational hobby. Grandpa and Grandma passed this quaint pastime along to their children, grandchildren and great-grandchildren.

One Sunday driving to Tintern, when I was mulling over the whole notion of a trigger, our sons were in the back seat carrying on a low-level argument about the number of Red-tailed Hawks they'd counted since leaving home. There it was; I smiled.

In an instant I knew exactly what I'd use as a reminder that'd activate a simple sentence. Red-tailed Hawks would be symbolic of the presence and protection of God, and upon seeing one I'd whisper a prayer: *Thank you, Lord, for your kind protection on my life.*

Later, when I told Anita, we decided to be intentional with the trigger. In doing so, it became evident that God uses it to bless and encourage us. We've noticed that, in times of difficulty or discouragement, there always seems to be a significant increase in the Red-tailed Hawk population wherever we happen to be.

When nature was in metamorphosis, with the leaves burning the landscape in dazzling shades of red, Grandpa Major's health began to rapidly deteriorate. It had been increasingly evident that his days on planet earth were coming to their natural conclusion, but seemingly overnight, he was weak, sick, and old. At eighty-six, he had always been the emotional rock of the family.

His grandchildren all thought he was indestructible. He was a man who understood better than most that life is a package deal that comes equipped with both joys and sorrows. It had been six years since the love of his life had passed away, and now he talked much about the past, sharing good and hard memories. He also sang or whistled the old hymns about heaven and life everlasting much more than usual.

One Saturday morning, I visited him. No one else was around, which was nice. We chatted about life. I told him some stories about our sons, and pride filled his eyes. I confessed about a prank that the Nice-guy Delinquents had pulled, with Maj and me involved. We'd built a dam in the big ditch, and we'd done such a first-rate job, a fair sized flood resulted. The neighborhood had been in an uproar over it for several days, but no one had ever been held accountable; we had gotten away with a rather large piece of mischief.

Grandpa looked at me and laughed loudly, dismissing it by saying that he'd known it had been us all along, but he wasn't going to rat out his own grandsons. He verbalized things about his feelings for me that I had never heard before, but always knew because he'd demonstrated them in so many different ways. He talked about my Dad and *that* terrible day. His voice broke when he said that having to be the one to identify the body was the single hardest thing he'd ever had to do. His face grimaced as the memory struck him anew. He started to describe the ugliness, but then stopped abruptly and smiled at me.

"It doesn't matter now," he said, forcing a feeble click-click. He stared off in the distance for a long moment. "Pretty soon nothing will matter to me."

"What do you mean?" I asked, not following him.

"I'm going home," he said with a calm assurance. "I'll see your Dad, Lawrie, and Grandma. No one knows how lonely it is here without her."

I bit my bottom lip and said nothing. There was heavy silence.

Grandpa was crying. "I can't fight anymore, Kenny," he said, tears streaming down his cheeks. "You don't think I'm a baby because I want to go home, do you?"

"No, Grandpa. I understand."

I'd always had esteem and admiration for him, but on that day, his stature grew even larger in my mind. As his physical body withered away, his life of faith had strength and vigor. For him, death wasn't the grim reaper or boogeyman lurking in the darkness waiting to snatch him away. Death was just the gateway to his eternal home of heaven.

On the second Sunday in November, which was destined to be his last time at church, he was standing in his usual spot in the foyer leaning heavily on his cane. He was slumped over, and the pain was obvious on his face and in his eyes. I went over, held his forearm for a moment, and asked how he was doing. His answer spoke volumes about his character and perseverance.

"I'm here, aren't I?"

I smiled and nodded. He did the same. An understanding passed between us; an understanding having to do with being the man of the family. I've thought about his stiff-necked determination many times.

It was incredible to witness, especially after the revelations about his health came to light. Four days later, Grandpa was taken away from the house he'd built with Grandma and became a patient at the Welland Hospital. It was then, when he was weakened and vulnerable, that we all found out for sure what many had suspected. Grandpa had been diagnosed with cancer a few years earlier, and rather than embarking on a course of treatment, he kept it to himself. He'd counted the cost in terms of dignity, then had sworn the doctor to secrecy.

Knowing my grandfather to be straightforward and outspoken, I can state categorically that his wishes would have been made clear beyond doubt. He then proceeded to live life, without chemotherapy or radiation, managing the intensifying pain as best he could with codeine and a vehement mental toughness.

The family sat vigil in shifts at the hospital. A week after he'd been admitted, he was ushered into glory. It was early in the morning, and as it happened, I was at his bedside with a cousin.

Grandpa's eyes were closed and had been for a long while. He was in a near comatose state, when suddenly his eyes popped open, he lifted his head off the pillow, and exclaimed in a strong voice, "I see heaven, I see Mom." He took one exuberant gasp of breath and shivered. The death rattles shook him tremendously, then he evacuated his earthen body and was gone. I held his hand and felt a warmness touch me. My lips pursed, and I said goodbye, then carefully closed my grandfather's eyes.

It was my privilege to say a few words at his funeral. In preparing them, I took his advice regarding homiletics to heart. Grandpa's wisdom was ingrained in me, "Say what you feel, feel what you say, and never let anyone but God tell you what to say." I wondered if there was any of his rare stuff inside me. His impact is stamped on whatever noble aspects are reflected in my character. I'm responsible for all defects and blemishes.

God's timing is always perfect. Grandpa had lived long enough to see the gears of redemption at work in my life, and somehow that provided much comfort. At my grandfather's graveside, my course was set. My intention was to continue to walk in obedience.

However, obedience is seldom easy. It can be a gravel road with potholes and dead-ends. And sometimes there are detours along the way that can get us lost or can be the locale where we toughen up, check our compass, and bear down. There's always more to learn, and endeavoring to be faithful brings no guarantees, except, of course, the one Jesus told his disciples, "In this world you will have trouble. But take heart, I have overcome the world."

It may be a harsh surprise, but sometimes the trouble comes because God leads us directly into disappointments. Sometimes God takes us into the wilderness to present challenges designed to change and refine us. In a sincere effort to be true to the white flag of surrender, I was soon to experience a barren place that'd be a crucible like no other.

5

Season of Comprehension

*"I remember my afflictions and my wandering, the bitterness
and the gall. I well remember them, and my soul is downcast
within me. Yet this I call to mind and therefore I have hope:
Because of the LORD's great love we are not consumed, for his
compassions never fail. They are new every morning: great is
your faithfulness."*

~Jeremiah~

"WHOSE IS THIS?" I asked, holding a cassette of *The Silver Tongued Devil And I* by Kris Kristofferson. It was January 1993, and I was in the cubby-hole office at Welland Stadium, home of the Welland Pirates. I was starting a new job selling advertising and doing promotional work, and this was my first day of employment.

The Assistant General Manager was eyeing me skeptically. I had picked the tape up off his desk. "Mine," he said, almost apologetically.

I laughed. "You and I are going to get along just fine."

All these years later that statement has proved itself out. His name was Jud, a native of Massachusetts, and along with being able to sing every song Hank Williams ever wrote, he's one of few people on the planet who relates to and understands my musical tastes.

While working together for the next six months we developed a substantial friendship. We had a connection that encompassed faith, worldview and, a peculiar appreciation for meaningful sad story-songs, which is a seldom seen trifecta. Sometimes, when most needed, God brings people into our lives for a season of encouragement, which is what occurred here, but in this case, the rich blessing expanded to a lifetime.

Everything was happening so fast now. We were living in the parsonage of the Port Colborne BIC Church. I was in transition, heading toward full-time ministry, but not quite there yet. Life was particularly busy, and it seemed that time was always running ahead of me. The internship had been progressing well and continued with increasing responsibilities and ever-present opportunities to learn. I scrambled to keep pace, which forced me to develop excellent time management skills and meant that the personal study program undertaking had me doing assignments on the fly.

The previous spring I'd written the doctrinal exam with surprising ease, and the feedback was mostly positive, though denominational potentates required me to do some extra reading on holiness, which, considering what I would soon be exposed to, was extremely ironic. That winter, we were having preliminary discussions with the bishop of the Midwest Conference about a church in Iowa.

Those deliberations were exciting, and I was likely far too anxious to have good objectivity. I was told that the church was eager to reach out to its community and grow, and that it required a pastor who appreciated Brethren in Christ history and heritage. Taking the words at face value, it was a no-brainer; it sounded like an appointment designed for my perspective and gift-mix.

Being inexperienced, and having been out of church circles for so long, I didn't recognize the code words or interpret the subtle nuance. In an interview process that included exchanging videotapes, we got to know each other a bit, then decided to take the next step.

Schedules were adjusted and arrangements made for Anita and me to fly to Des Moines to further explore the possibilities with the folks in Dallas Center. We did so on a weekend in February, and at the time, David Koresh and the Branch Davidians were making national headlines from their compound in Waco, TX.

The fact that a tortured theology was in the news made an interesting backdrop for dialogue that included much emphasis on doctrinal issues and the imperative of being grounded in God's Word. I heard many testimonies about the all-sufficient nature of the Bible, which on the surface no one could offer a legitimate argument against, but I would discover that their reading was singularly literal.

During a group Q & A, I had to provide rather detailed exegesis of my understanding of eschatology. Eschatology is the theological term for dealing with matters concerning the end of the world as we know it. This emphasis on end times should have caused the hackles to rise on my discernment so that I'd scratch a bit deeper, but not so. Being somewhat naïve in thinking that this potential position would be the only option available to me, I glossed over any concerns and missed seeing what should have been clear to a one-eyed blind man.

At the end of the weekend visit, we had a decision to make that had a certain frightful quality to it. The difficulty of logistics seemed impossible to me. There were miles and miles of governmental red-tape to be unraveled. There were fees and expenses that had to be covered; there were family dynamics to be considered. There were pushes and pulls from a vast variety of voices. I downplayed the distance with a shrug, but fact is, we'd be relocating over nine hundred miles away.

It's not an exact science to determine what all is required in the realm of obedience, and it's even feasible that our channels can get clogged up regardless of our willingness to hear and understand.

In this instance, we sweated out the details and made every sincere effort to ascertain the correct response. We sought God's direction and guidance. We listened to the counsel of brothers and sisters. We tested and prayed and asked what we thought were all the right and relevant questions, then committed to the sense of call with all the energy and enthusiasm we possessed.

In June 1993, Anita and I were fired up and full of high hopes as we readied ourselves to be the pastoral couple at the Mound Park BIC Church. We packed our belongings and moved to Dallas Center, Iowa. Our two oldest sons stayed behind. The oldest one would be heading off to England for a six month stint with Operation Mobilization later that summer. The second oldest had a job working concessions at Welland Stadium and would join us in August.

The leaving was bittersweet; thrilling and exciting because of the adventure awaiting us, but pulling up stakes meant having to deal with lots of goodbyes. The Port Colborne Church took a page out of Cecil B. DeMille and put on a full-blown production for a going away service. There were smiles and laughter, along with plenty of tears and tender moments, and much well-wishing and prayers, all of which we cherished.

≈ ≈ ≈

On the morning of the installation service at the Mound Park Church, I was jarred out of any possible rose-colored idealism that might have been present. In an adult Sunday School class held in the sanctuary, a symptom of a noxious sickness was easily diagnosed.

The teacher was a forceful and dogmatic man who exhorted the small group in an emotive voice that at some junctures pitched upward into a bellow. His Scripture was King David's prayer of repentance in Psalm 51, but it was entirely unrecognizable to me. He dug vitriol and judgment out of the psalmist's cries for mercy. He managed to transform David's heartfelt plea for cleansing into a vindictive homily that heaped large doses of guilt and shame on his listeners. His attacking style was as offensive as his abuse and mishandling of the text.

I glanced around at the regulars in the class and was shocked by their reaction. No one even blinked. Some were smiling and nodding in agreement. It came to me that this wasn't out of the ordinary; this was the norm. I sat there chewing on my bottom lip thinking that, if I was a visitor, I'd get up and leave, then on the heels of that thought was the idea that, in an hour or so, I'd officially be the pastor of this church.

We'd willingly uprooted ourselves to serve God by caring for and endeavoring to help a congregation reach its full potential, but soon discouragement would be a perpetual motion treadmill. From that first morning on, discernment was on high alert. It didn't take long to determine that the congregation was on life-support; in reality, that is being generous. The church had a rich legacy in the denomination, but now its terminal illness had reduced it to a skeletal frame consumed by tales of yesteryear.

It was actually quite sad to eyewitness its thrashing around and lashing out to protect and preserve itself. At its peak, in the nineteen fifties and sixties, it'd been dynamic and thriving, a truly healthy and sending congregation, but it settled at a plateau and became self-satisfied and inward focused. Some bad theology was perpetuated and exacerbated by the long-standing closed-community culture of sects in the Dallas Center community that had far too much impact and influence on the personality and character of the church.

Outward appearances were always a motivation for behavior; a near obsessive concern with what the Old Order River Brethren or Dunkard Brethren might think imprisoned the Mound Park congregation. It was 1993, and I was a grown man who'd been up and down and all around, but somehow my education in bitter legalism had been sorely lacking, which was quickly remedied.

While playing catch with our sons in the back yard on a hot Saturday afternoon I was spotted wearing shorts, which evidently was strictly forbidden. Imagine our shocked surprise when Anita and I had a special visit from a stalwart member to be lectured about the evils of that attire and the necessity to set a good example and preach a dress code. No BIC pastor could ever wear shorts in that town and neither could any member of their family. That incident occurred on our second weekend there, but it was only the beginning of my enlightenment.

I was to learn a whole host of supposed spiritual truths about buttons and zippers, and all manner of clothing. Some of the stories have near hilarious elements to them, but the humor vanishes with the realization of the tragic bondage that result when human-centric wisdom and reasoning is elevated to a high pedestal.

The congregation had compiled a lengthy agenda of dissension. That, along with its particular brand of legalism, created a toxic quality in the body, with factions continually vying for power and control.

A newcomer almost required a program to keep track of who was talking to whom, and who was on the outs. Divisions were starkly defined, but allegiances seemed to be always shifting, with all sides praying to the same God and quoting Scripture from the same book to justify their positions.

It was all quite disconcerting. I found myself always in the middle, trying to hear and understand all sides, but much of it was entirely incomprehensible. Some of the grievances went back twenty years or more, but were spoken about as though it'd only been yesterday or last week.

The most aggressive coalition was the one that saw themselves as champions of pure BIC doctrine. It was solidly entrenched. They were the faithful remnant and were determined to safeguard what they perceived to be essential. Their concept of having a pastor who appreciated BIC history and heritage meant one who would comply with their perception of the doctrine of holiness, which was about pattern of dress and behavior rooted in the nineteenth century.

Holiness had been strained to the point of becoming unhinged. Here, for anyone who came into their assembly, it was the expectation that external expressions motivated the heart. In fact, genuine holiness transpires when we inwardly yield to God and are open to the Holy

Spirit's mysterious work which transforms our heart little by little and bit by bit. The result is progressive outward changes in lifestyle or perspective that honors God.

If false gods are defined as anything that diverts devotion and attention away from the Creator and his redemptive purposes in the world, then their glorification of the bygone days of BIC practices crept astonishingly close to idolatry. I write that with great pain. It was extremely sad because the individuals were misguided but well-meaning in their desire to be faithful.

Once upon a time the church had been alive and well, actively involved in impacting their community and planting gospel seeds, but by the time I arrived on the scene the residue of that vibrancy was all that remained. It'd mutated into deadness that was emotionally and spiritually destructive. Pastoral families had a short shelf life in Dallas Center. For over fifteen years the average tenure had been three years and out.

Two months into our journey, while standing near the door at the close of the service, I received a hundred dollar handshake accompanied by an admonition to preach *real* holiness. I thought the man was just kidding around, and I started to thank him, but the fiery gleam in his eyes made my mouth stop working because I realized he was serious. I mumbled something and shrugged, and that was where it was left.

I felt dirty; I wanted to get rid of the money quickly. We were leaving for Roxbury Camp in Pennsylvania immediately after church, where I would be taking a course as part of the ongoing requirements of the credentialing process. The drive was eighteen or nineteen hours long, which allowed me to vent and try to figure out how to feel or think about the mess we found ourselves in. Anita participated in the debriefing session, and her conclusions were as grim as mine.

The first time the offering bucket was passed at camp, I dug the balled up wad of the hundred dollar bill out of my pocket and tossed it in; I wanted nothing to do with it. I prayed that God would give me clear direction as to how to proceed.

We shared what was happening with some trusted friends, and that was helpful. By the time we were heading back to Iowa, deep in my heart I knew that one of two things was going to happen; either God was going to perform the biggest miracle since the resurrection of Christ, or we were going to bury a long dead body.

We carried a burden, developed a vision, and threw ourselves into the effort, all the while praying for breakthroughs that would facilitate the miracle. We tried traditional approaches, but were also bold and creative, taking risks and chances. Nothing had any effect. Here was a sick cell in the body of Christ that required a radical transformational turnaround, and without that, it needed to get out of the church business.

Comprehension came to me in a moment of astounding clarity. It was clear that malignant dysfunctions had taken years to develop into a spiritual carcinoma that infected everyone it touched. It was equally clear that what had come to pass to me personally when I closed myself off to God and spat at grace was mirrored in the corporate body of the Mound Park BIC Church. It reflected the ugliness of my life in exile, which drilled home a truth that impaled me.

Churches are nothing more than collections of deeply flawed people who lug around their garbage while attempting to experience transcendence and meaning. Choices have consequences, for individuals and for churches. Slamming the door shut on the continuous work of God in any area of our lives will sooner or later have negative impact on our well-being.

No one can say no to God with impunity; not individuals and not churches. Some of our worst troubles result from our stubborn determination to make decisions and do as we please without regard for the dictates of Scripture.

Fortunately for us, Christ is building *his* church, and God accommodates our faithless and feckless nature by bestowing grace, which we desperately need all of the time. Our urgency for it becomes exquisite when waters are rising and our feet are entangled in the weeds.

In those difficult times, the faithfulness of God is so real as to be almost tangible, which is entirely experiential, but when it fell to me to preside over the death and burial of the Mound Park BIC Church, grace touched me in that distinct manner. Two years after arriving energized by a high-octane passion to accomplish something for the Kingdom, it became my responsibility to officiate at the funeral service for the church.

Metaphorical or not, it was one more casket that I had to stand beside. Funerals are seldom cheery affairs, and let me assure you that a funeral for a church is devastating to everyone involved.

Dallas Center was a desert for me, an isolated town surrounded by acre after acre of corn and soybeans. The difficulties took me to the precipice of my limits, and it was there that the full flower of my frailty withered on its vine. My self-reliance was burned up and melted down to be reshaped into a pragmatic faith that applied practical dependence on the One who held the future in his hands. He could do with me as he pleased because my life belonged to him. My life was about what God desired to do in and through me, and here's the shocking tripwire--he can do whatsoever he pleases.

Those are tough lessons that must be relearned on a regular basis, but it was at Dallas Center that I first began to grasp their far-reaching meaning and ramifications. In that barren place I completed the personal study program. While doing so, I routinely experienced agonizing ministry situations that weren't covered in any textbooks. I was operating on guts and instinct. It could have been too long in the wasteland, but instead, given my wiring, I received an incredible education.

It wasn't all hardships. Sure, there were tears, but those served to make the laughter all the more intense. In mid-February 1994, God provided a shot of grace disguised as family and friends. Our oldest son had completed his assignment with Operation Mobilization and was spending several weeks with us. His anecdotes and unrelenting sense of humor lifted the gloom surrounding us, which was good. He also upgraded the church's music ministry greatly. Ken had been playing guitar since he was eight years old, and like many musicians, worked hard at making it look real easy. He returned from England with a harmonica, on which he had become quite proficient.

At my urging he performed retooled versions of old folk-rock tunes he'd heard all his life; his subtle change of phrasing elevated spiritual songs to an even more meaningful level. I doubt anyone in the congregation had any inkling as to who'd penned the originals, because if they would have, our customary tension and conflicts would have increased immeasurably.

As it was, we were dealing with a tangled up web so out of sync with conventional behavior that eventually I'd have to rattle the chain of command to seek help, but those details will be shared a little further along in the story.

While enjoying every stolen moment of family time with our four sons all together, Jud happened by with his friend Kevin and stopped in for a visit. They were on a cross-country jam session, performing in whatever venue available while on a mission to discover what middle America thought about Jesus.

Traveling from town to town, they'd hang out wherever people gathered to survey strangers with a single question: "Who is Jesus?" They recorded the answers on cassette tapes and were enjoying the project immensely.

By the time Jud and Kevin arrived in Dallas Center they had rambled across the Deep South and were working their way north and east. Some of their findings were fascinating. Those tapes revealed a multi-faced portrait of Jesus that was imaginative and largely human-centric in nature.

They were with us over a weekend, so I recruited them for a Sunday morning mini-concert. I didn't have to put a hammerlock on them at all; they were more than willing. Ken joined them, and what followed was truly an incredibly rich time worthy of having been filmed, but sadly no one had any video cameras rolling.

That staid congregation sat in stiff resolve as the first chords were strummed, but then as the music swelled into a contagion it lifted them out of their no-nonsense dignity and had them responding with foot-loose enthusiasm. There was even some hooting and hollering in old-style holiness fashion as the trio performed bluesy roots gospel, complete with wailing harmonica and twangy guitars.

It was all a tremendous blessing. It met me at my point of need and gave me a boost in confidence which at that moment was so necessary. I came to be secure in the knowledge that no matter how twisted the ongoing downward spiral might become, I was going to survive. It might get ugly and dicey, with pieces of me shredded, but the bits would get put back together again.

As I told you, when Jud was introduced, sometimes God brings people into our lives for simple reasons of encouragement. Sometimes we need that special kinship to rise above and overcome the troubles.

Speaking of kinship, in March 1994, there was an episode in southwest Oklahoma that involved some vulture bait and a famed buffalo hunter, which at some juncture deserves its own literary forum, but now is not the time or place. I mention it here because the oasis in those desert years was relational.

While serving in Dallas Center, I came in contact with a handful of men whom I refer to as my Kansas Brethren. It was a network of pastors in the Midwest Conference. I plugged in and was enriched by the relationships. We intentionally kept in contact to support and care for each other.

It was an honor to be invited and included from the very beginning. Mostly it was phone calls or notes, but twice annually we'd hole up in a hotel room for a few days of purposeful prayer. We'd share war stories from the battlefront and compare notes, exchanging ideas and suggestions. There were also always healthy doses of amusing antidotes that'd have us howling and gasping.

I remember those times with joy because the relationships kept me alive. My Kansas Brethren performed the spiritual equivalent of mouth to mouth resuscitation on more than one occasion.

The final service of the Mound Park BIC Church was a Sunday in August. It was one of those hot and sticky dog days. With the thermostat set low the air conditioner was working incessantly, but the cooling currents could do nothing to alleviate the tension in the old building. Every face was lined with anxiety.

The elderly ladies who made up the core of the congregation were clustered together and trying to smile, but the strain of the day was too much. It had all happened so fast. They'd invested their lives in the work of the church and now, in less than a month, decisions had been made which resulted in its closure.

From the opening Scripture to the final hymn the inevitable uneasiness kept the proceedings on edge. In the view of many in the group, I was the catalyst who'd caused these sad circumstances. I was the bad guy, which I suppose, had some merit from their perspective, though I could never agree with that assessment. I was merely endeavoring to complete a natural process.

The church that had grown, developed, and ministered out of the building on Hatton Street in Dallas Center had lived its life. After it had ceased to be a healthy, functioning body, administrators of the denomination did everything possible and applied extraordinary measures in attempts to revive it, but that was not to be.

Funerals can be delayed, but not denied; funerals are the culmination of a life lived. Just as people have a life cycle, so do churches. They are born; they have a life full of hopes, dreams, and accomplishments along with despairs, frustrations, and failures. Then death, natural or not, comes knocking.

It was painful to bury the Mound Park Church. It was hurtful. Feelings of futility piled up, and became so heavy I wanted nothing more than to escape, but couldn't because life does what it does. We must accept it and press on. Our responsibility as believers is to honor God by being faithful.

God's grace is a multifaceted wonder. The funeral service concluded in a muted celebration of communion. There were tears, hugs, and collective sorrow.

Early that afternoon, Anita and I traveled to Abilene, KS. Wesley and Jonathan were there hanging out with friends. The heat was stifling, and our 1984 Oldsmobile station-wagon did not have air conditioning. All the windows were down. The rushing wind combined with the radio playing loud, made it noisy and not conducive to conversation.

It was a six hour drive and for the first half of it we were mostly silent, letting each other sort through jumbled emotions. I drew strength from Anita's quiet resolve. She was convinced that everything was going to be fine. God would provide for us as he always had. In this she was certain.

I, on the other hand, was going to need some convincing. A sense that God had abandoned us was creeping through me. I wanted to rage at God, to scream and rant, but squelched it with a bleak determination.

A couple miles west of Kansas City on Interstate 70, I spotted a Red-tailed Hawk sitting on a fence post. It was the trigger that was supposed to remind me of an attribute of God's character. My mind jumped to the automatic prayer, with the words beginning to take shape, but I refused to pray.

Several miles later there was another Red-tailed Hawk perched on a railing. Like the first one, it was on the left side of the highway. I glanced at Anita to determine if she had seen it. She gave no indication that she had.

The miles were gobbled up, and I began to puzzle over what was happening. There were Red-tailed Hawk sightings at regular intervals. I wondered if it was really taking place or if I was imagining the birds.

They were always on the driver's side of the road, sitting tall and out in the open like solitary sentinels or guardians.

It was freaky. Despite the muggy weather, a chill chased up my spine. In a phrase left over from the hippy-dippy seventies, the hawks were *weirding me out*.

I noted the odometer and started marking the distance between the birds. The hawks were showing up on fence posts or railings every couple miles. The familiar words of the prayer kept trying to form, but I effectively knocked them apart. Crushed by the weight of burying a church, and wanting so much to gripe and complain to God, my heart was in turmoil.

I couldn't believe what I was seeing. Denial seemed like a good place to go. Then, when another hawk appeared, Anita broke the silence between us with an observation.

"That's at least a dozen," she said softly.

Frowning, I turned off the radio. "What?"

"That's at least a dozen Red-tailed Hawks."

"You see them too?" I asked, swallowing dryly.

"Why haven't you said anything?"

I forced a smile. "Why haven't you?"

She grinned. "They've all been on your side of the road."

Tears formed and spilled down my cheek. "Thank you, Lord, for your kind protection on my life," I prayed in a frail and quavering voice. I exhaled a burst of air.

Anita repeated the prayer with a firmness that steeled me. She reached over, held my hand and said, "Everything is going to be okay. We'll get through all of this."

Calmness settled on me. I squeezed her hand. Instead of *weirding me out*, now the birds of prey gave me comfort and hope. God was breaking into the troubled discouragement in a tangible way to make us aware of his presence in our lives.

For the rest of the way, we purposefully watched, and saw an exceptional number of Red-tailed Hawks. There was even one atop the Abilene exit sign. We both laughed.

≈ ≈ ≈

A few days before we pulled out to put Dallas Center far behind us, I received a phone call from one of my Kansas Brethren, a redeemed old rocker named Ron who consistently rallied the troops and led the charge.

"Hey, Ken. Just wanted to check in and see how you're doing."

"Thanks, Ron. I'm okay, I think."

"Come on, man. You have to be hurting."

"Yeah," I admitted, more to myself than to him. "I think I'm done."

"Packing you mean?"

"No. Done with ministry. I'm finished."

"Really?" he asked, his voice rising. "Are you sure about that?"

"I answered the call, man. Now it's over."

Ron chuckled. "I wouldn't bet on it if I were you."

"It sure feels like it's all over. I got nothing left."

"Listen to me," he said sternly. "If you had prepared to be a doctor, then your first patient was dead on arrival, would you stop practicing medicine?"

"I supposed not," I muttered, lips pursed.

After hanging up, I stared at the phone for a long time. I appreciated Ron's words of encouragement, but at some level, wished he had not posed the question. I felt all used up.

That conversation stayed with me. The implications of his illustration about preparing to be a doctor would nip at me in morose or moody moments. Whenever the notion of tossing in the towel on the call to ministry entered my mind, the imagery of his words would taunt me.

My first pastorate had been DOA. It was riddled with failures, but time would prove that in this gut-wrenching season of comprehension, God had planted the seeds for what he'd prepared for me down the road a ways.

In early September 1995, we returned to southern Ontario. It was an uneventful cross-country journey that became a patience stretching shuffle through the mazelike bureaucracy of Canada Customs. The debacle at the border in Windsor has extremely funny elements in the distance of years, but as it was happening, it had all the humor of an amputation.

We had been in contact with Canada Customs and had filled out all the necessary paperwork. Anita had diligently given attention to every detail according to what she'd been told in numerous phone conversations, but it didn't matter. We were ambushed by some gung-ho regulators determined to uphold every potential requirement in the rule book.

Contrary to what we had been told over the phone regarding specifics, there were taxes to be paid, importation fees to be satisfied, and various other financial obligations that were outrageous, and I still don't understand much of it. When all the tallying up was completed, we had to hand over almost a thousand dollars, which was most of the funds we'd squirreled away to reestablish ourselves.

For over a month we lived out of boxes, staying with friends in Welland who were truly a blessing to us. For awhile I hoped for an employment opportunity in ministry, but it quickly became evident that there'd be no such opening occurring anytime soon, which was likely good because I was physically, emotionally and spiritually exhausted, beat up, frustrated, discouraged; as close to certifiable defeat as I ever want to be again. There was no exclusive target on which to focus my angst, so being an equal opportunity person, I aimed my frustration and anger at God, denominational leadership, and myself.

An old farmhouse on the property owned by Niagara Christian College in Fort Erie was made available to us. I was back driving cab in Welland, and Anita had gotten a job with AWANA International in Fonthill, so the daily commute was long, but the rent fit our strained-to-the-max budget.

I plugged along in my faith, but had begun wisecracking that I was out of the reverend business, and for me it was no joke. I was accepting the slow realization that I may have blown my shot at it. I put the grief over my journey at Dallas Center behind me and moved on.

The sorrow did what sorrow does when left unattended; it festered in me. Without even realizing it, I defaulted to the familiar behavior and mindset patterns of isolation and alienation. Robotic precision was in play as I put up internal barriers and withdrew into myself, but thankfully, God had things to do in me and would be faithful.

One of the daily runs I had that autumn was picking up a six-year-old Down Syndrome child in the east end of Welland to take him to Quaker Road School on the far north side of the city. His name was Dustin. He was sweet, quiet and well-behaved, and despite the hard crust of my gruff appearance, I typically connect well with children.

After the usual stand-offish hesitancy, I did so with Dustin. He would get strapped into the passenger seat beside me, and we'd hold hands and make funny noises together which would set off the giggles in him.

On an ordinary morning drenched in sunshine, while taking him to his special education class, we were sitting at an intersection along with a long line of cars.

I was silently grouching because the driver in front of me had weaved in and out of traffic, cutting off two other cars in an attempt to beat the red light, but there he sat waiting, one whole car length closer to his destination.

Apparently he had gotten his license as a prize in a box of Cracker Jack. As the sarcastic rant inside me was gathering itself into its swirling second wind, a still small voice gagged it by asserting itself: *Sing Jesus Loves Me to Dustin*. I sputtered out a grunt of a laugh, refusing it immediately. The words were repeated a little more insistently, which resulted in me stiffening my resolve to resist it.

One would think that, because of past experiences, I'd respond to that kind of prompting with distinct obedience, but not so.

Sometimes a thickness blankets me, and I can be uncommonly obtuse, plus there's a preponderance of evidence that I possess a mammoth stubbornness, so there's no sense in attempting to deny it. My jaw tightened. As the light turned green and we started moving, I considered the words and wondered why my split-second response had been so harsh.

In this case, there was a beastly bit of truth that until that moment I hadn't even imagined. All the pain and heartbreak of my first venture into pastoral ministry was filling my soul with bitterness. I felt abandoned by God. I had done everything to answer the call; I had jumped through every hoop and had given it the best I had to offer, with nothing to show for it all other than acute feelings of failure.

Here's the most unpleasant piece of truth that crystallized in my mind. At this low-point I wasn't real sure that Jesus loved me. How could I sing it to a little boy?

Cruising along, there it was again: *Sing Jesus Loves Me to Dustin*. This time, however, it struck me with the sting of a willow switch snapped across the back of my legs, and I caved in. I reached over and took hold of Dustin's hand. I made sure I had his attention, and then in a wavering off-key rasp starting singing. Keeping my attention on the road, I shot furtive glances at him as I enunciated each word and tried my best to hit all the right notes.

Dustin tilted his head curiously and smiled a smile that kept getting bigger and brighter as I sang. By the time I got to the chorus, there were tears behind my dark sunglasses and my voice was straining:
"Yes, Jesus loves me!
Yes, Jesus loves me!
Yes, Jesus loves me!
The Bible tells me so."

I pulled to the curb and had a moment with Dustin that was deeply spiritual. His smile was beaming up from deep within. A chill of recognition contradicted the warmth of the day; I knew that Dustin knew Jesus loved him; in that transfixed instant, I also knew Jesus loved me.

After delivering Dustin to school, I took a call and, when finished with it, found a secluded spot along the Welland Canal and had a good cry and a long talk with God in which I vented the poison. In the terminology of the church, I prayed through and had assurance that God was still on the throne and drawing all things together in my life for his plans and purposes.

Life continued, and we slipped into the routine of it. Anita and I were involved in lay ministry at the Port Colborne Church, and the efforts were often fulfilling. I had resigned myself to the idea that there'd never be another pastorate for me, but a near-desperate desire had been entombed beneath that resignation. At Niagara Camp 1996, that sense of loss was going to crawl out from under and make itself heard.

The second evening, the speaker preached from the passage in Luke where a group of disciples had been fishing all night and caught nothing. They were busily cleaning their nets when along came Jesus. He told them to go out into the deep water and cast their nets again. Peter resisted with knee-jerk predictability, and it was at this point that I checked out.

In my mind, I engaged in a gripe-filled diatribe of bellyaching that surely made Peter's complaints pale in comparison. I unloaded with every criticism and objection I had, but God didn't recoil from my whiny protestations. Rather, he gently reminded me of a gut-level prayer of surrender on an April morning not so long ago, and I listened, coming to a fresh awareness of the open-ended nature of obedience.

By the end of the service, it was profoundly clear that as far as God was concerned I wasn't out of the reverend business. I needed to cast my nets again.

That night, while the stars shone brightly and fireflies darted to and fro, Anita and I sat on the front porch of the farmhouse, talking and praying for quite awhile. There was so much to examine, so many factors to place into consideration that it was daunting to me, but God had brought us together, and we filled in each other's weakness with strength.

Once again her practicality and unyielding expression of simple faith steeled me for the task. There was one new issue in our life that we both attempted to do a little linguistic dance around before acknowledging it. Our daughter-in-law was expecting our first grandchild in November. It was an exciting time full of hope and promise.

I had blurred through or messed up so much about fatherhood, and though it's counterintuitive to grace and forgiveness, my failings nagged at me. Somewhere deep within there was this unconscious and unspoken yearning for a shot at redemption as a grandfather. Does that sound like convoluted reasoning?

Perhaps it was and is, but in reality, sometimes our spirit is fully willing to embrace the healing and mystical aspects of God's love, but our flesh is far too weak to do so. It's part of what it means to be human.

I voiced this overwhelming idea that night, and Anita offered encouragement and understanding, of which she seems to have an endless supply. Together, we laid the issue before God in the context of actively seeking a pastoral ministry position. A peace settled on the discussion and, before finally going to bed, we decided on a plan. I'd put my resume together and have it all ready to be sent out the day our grandchild was born.

We would trust God with our concerns and desires, and step out in faith by making ourselves available to several different conferences, with a decision fixed that we were willing to go anywhere east of the Mississippi River. We're not privy to what occurs in the heavenlies, but given my present perspective, I suspect that when we issued that caveat, God likely had a rip-roaring laugh.

November 3rd was a Sunday. Michael was in his first year at Messiah College. He had traveled home on Friday for the intent purpose of not missing out on the big event. He wanted to be with his older brother when his niece or nephew was born. They called early to tell us our daughter-in-law had been in labor most of the night, and they were taking her to the hospital.

I was doing pulpit supply that morning at Riverside Chapel. I had one of those hilarious opening stories that get filed away for future use because of its universal appeal, but this particular one hasn't been dusted off in years. I preached myself dry, then we rushed home to wolf down some lunch and pick up the stack of resumes in their signed, sealed, and stamped envelopes. We delivered them to a mailbox on our way to the hospital.

The afternoon disappeared in a haze of waiting, then in the early evening, Zoe Grace was born. By the time she hollered her way into the world, I'd left the hospital to take Michael to Fort Erie to connect with his ride back to college. He missed being present for his niece's birth by about an hour.

That night I was overcome by a powerful need to pray for my granddaughter. I followed through, then decided to fast the next day and pray for her. While doing so, I took my cab for a little out of the way trip to Grimsby and stopped in at the hospital to visit. Holding her for the first time was awesome, which I know is cliché, but allow me to assure you that if cradling a newborn baby doesn't inspire awe in one's heart, there are issues present that no cardiac surgeon could ever rectify regardless of his or her skill.

Of course, she was beautiful; a little chub-chub with high cheekbones and red hair. Nowadays we have two beautiful granddaughters; the redheaded young lady and her brunette sister, Jessica Noel, a brown-eyed sweetie who has a giggle that's magical. I often wonder how an old ugly mug like me gets to be surrounded by such beauties. Just lucky, I guess. Or more accurately, just blessed.

In the next two weeks, while my resume made its way through the postal maze, I began fasting regularly, and it came to me that I needed to pursue God's direction in this manner. Not knowing exactly what decision to make while wanting to get it right means seeking God with an increased intensity. I did so in these days and sketched out a plan to be deliberate about it over the next number of months. It came in a flash of inspiration.

The strategy was to make every effort to eat healthy and begin to progressively increase physical activity. Extended times of fasting were integrated into the schedule. The premeditated course was about never underestimating the power of prayer. It had a definite beginning and a projected conclusion on Easter Sunday, March 30, 1997.

It became known to me as a journey of grace because every aspect of it was bathed in prayer as I kept dragging the same three questions before the throne of grace: *Who am I? Where am I going? What does God require of me?*

One evening in late November, just after implementing my plan, I received a phone call that'd keep me motivated to pursue it to its ending. Hearing from God and getting it right was overwhelmingly essential to me. As much as one may want to, we can never eliminate the human factor in making decisions, but my bull-dog grit was determined to give it my best shot. The call came from the bishop of what was then known as Central Conference, the five states of Ohio, Michigan, Wisconsin, Indiana and Illinois.

Bishop John was the only reason we'd even sent our resume that far away. It was risky, but we had determined that there were several churches in Michigan or northern Ohio that fit our requirement to be relatively close to our grandbaby. He had a rather large reputation in the denomination, which I'd heard enough about to know that I admired him. I had actually witnessed his style first-hand when our paths crossed while getting embroiled in relational foolishness in Dallas Center. He was serving as Director of Bishops at the time.

A messed up situation materialized that was beyond my breadth of knowledge and far above my pay grade. It was a display of passive-aggressive one-upmanship that was downright hurtful. There were no case studies or examples to follow in any of the textbooks.

After mulling it over without coming to any conclusion, I contacted my immediate superior and sought his advice. Bishop Glenn gave me a fair hearing, then after an uncomfortable silence on the line, confessed that he'd never heard of such a thing. Somehow that made me feel better. Maybe I wasn't losing my mind. He commiserated with me, then said he wanted to consult his boss, who had a wealth of training in conflict resolution. He'd get back to me.

In my gut, I wanted to confront the situation with toughness, but was hesitant because of the absurdity of the circumstance and my inexperience. I was worried that my carnality had gotten out of its corral and was running free. However, when Bishop Glenn called back, he told me that he'd conveyed the tale of woe up the chain of command and there'd been in-depth discussions. The official response from the Director of Bishops surprised me because of its forthright and unwavering approach to the problem.

Bishop John advocated a face-to-face directness which was much more vigorous and inflexible than the hard line I wanted to draw. He cautioned care as regarding ego and pride, saying that this all had to be done with the greatest manifestation of tough love. He even provided a set of options on how to proceed, which all made sense, and also affirmed that my instincts had been correct. It wasn't unfettered carnality to expect adult human beings who professed faith to be responsible for their actions.

If I hadn't gone through that meat-grinder of ministry, I would have never had the opportunity to be impressed by Bishop John's character and approach to leadership. The Central Conference would have never received my resume; we sent it only out of respect for Bishop John.

That evening on the phone, he wanted to talk about a church in Illinois, which immediately was a caution sign simply because of the distance. I waved at Anita and she came over beside me as I listened. He gave me all the information he had, pulling no punches and not glazing it with sugar at all. He was blunt, which I appreciated.

There had been a chaotic break-up between the congregation and its last pastor; he had been fired. I scribbled that on the pad I was making notes on and underlined it three times, motioning to Anita to see it. She wrinkled her brow and shrugged noncommittally. I asked how that had happened, and he told me straight. He said that he thought it could have been handled much more cleanly, but that the pastor had indeed been terminated. Firing a pastor, when there was no moral failure involved, wasn't a fact easily dismissed.

That episode alone gave me pause, plus, not being geographically impaired, I knew exactly where Illinois was on the map. I was beginning to think of how I could graciously say thanks but no thanks. We talked for nearly three-quarters of an hour, and the dialogue wound down with him asking if I'd be willing to have a conference call with the Pastoral Search Committee. Talking on the phone from the comfort of our living room surrounded by my books didn't sound too difficult, so I gave my consent. I figured if I flatly refused it, I'd always be curious about these people who had expressed interest in me based on my resume, some words I'd written, marking up good clean paper.

"Have we got a map of Illinois?" I asked, hanging up.

"Yes," Anita said, hurrying out of the room. She returned momentarily, and we unfolded it on my desk and began searching for the town. It took a long while to find it and, when we did, we looked at each other with disbelief. There it was, Morrison, west of Chicago, and if my thumb measurements were accurate, about twelve miles east of the Mississippi River.

We checked and double-checked it, and eventually even dug out a ruler to confirm the distance. Either we simply couldn't believe it or the irony was too much for us to grasp. We laughed, but not the kind that comes as a result of humor, but rather, this was tinged by bewilderment. *We were willing to go anywhere east of the Mississippi River.* The lesson? It's never a good idea to give God an ultimatum or put restrictions on obedience.

We included our sons in the decision-making process. Ken was married and living in St. Catharines with his wife and daughter; Michael was a freshman in college; Wesley was a sophomore in high school; Jonathan was in junior high. There were many mixed feelings expressed. We listened, processed, and talked through it all step by step.

One of the serious concerns was whether or not this was a sick church that'd chew us up and spit us out. The idea that the church had given their previous pastor the old heave-ho troubled everyone. We hashed it over and over. It could be an indicator of a latent illness or that something had gone dreadfully wrong in the relationship, which made us wonder about the personalities involved.

The conference call happened, and everyone was positive about going forward, which would mean a face-to-face interview during a weekend visit to Morrison. That was scheduled for late January. Wesley and Jonathan would join us for the trip. The family consensus was that if there was any whiff of sickness, we'd back away in an almighty hurry, but, if it was a healthy church that'd mismanaged problems to a dismal ending, we'd have to be open to God.

Through all of this I pursued the spiritual quest begun after the birth of our granddaughter.

It consisted of eliminating junk food from my diet, while increasing my intake of fruits and vegetables. In all actuality I was merely putting into practice what I'd learned about nutrition in elementary school. A simple phrase became a motto: Eat less, eat healthy, and move more.

I began walking every day, short distances at first because that was all I could manage, but gradually three, four, and five miles at a time. Sometimes these took on the character of forced marches, but they were prayer walks. With expectations of getting answers, I kept presenting myself to God repeating those three questions and asking for specific guidance.

After twenty years of neglect and lots of abuse, my body responded slowly at first, but then as muscle grew and fat disappeared, I began noticing dramatic changes. The pain in the left hip had been a constant companion for so long that it had to be of the extreme variety for me to even acknowledge it. Then I'd scowl and grumble some, and swallow a small handful of extra-strength pain medication.

The journey of grace provided me with much of what I had sought. The discoveries were self-enlightening, and I wrote the conclusions down to hold myself accountable to them. I carry that paper around in my briefcase and have pulled it out to reconsider it many times, which often challenges me anew. Most of the details are personal and private, between God and me, but some can be shared here.

Who am I? In many ways I'm a walking contradiction, the quintessence of the Apostle Paul's moral struggles in Romans seven or the prophet Isaiah's dilemma experienced in the year King Uzziah died. I remain a coarse and profane man saved and sustained by the marvelous grace of God.

Where am I going? Long-term I'm still eagerly heading toward that destination, and truly hope and pray that it won't be a horizon too far for me to reach. Under the short-term category, it was definitely the Morrison BIC Church.

What does God require of me? Nothing more or less than he requires of any disciple, but since we're each unique, my answer has demands that are custom-fit to the quirks of my personality.

In June 1997, once again we packed a Ryder truck and launched out on a new adventure. The Morrison BIC Church was a perfect match for us. It was like a dovetail joint coming together, and I'm not sure I'll ever experience a better or tighter fit.

We connected from the beginning. From our first visit until we finally said our goodbyes over a decade later, I always had the sense that God was using all the junk and garbage in my past to grow me stronger and help others. For the most part, they were open to every nutty idea for outreach I presented. Once the endeavor was put into action, they'd pour themselves into it. I often referred to them as the hardest working congregation on the planet, which wasn't hyperbole.

I could fill pages with stories about friendships of the life-long variety that were forged, but suffice it to say that our ten and a half years there are looked upon with fondness. I found kindred spirits haunting places like the Fenton Bunker, Lyndon Pub, Victory Center or Beans, Books & Beliefs. I hung out with a shifting cast of interesting characters who had no illusions about the truth of God or the mixed nut bag of human nature.

There were programmers, painters, doctors, nurses, welders, farmers, tradesmen, teachers, administrators, engineers, machinists, groomers, grinders, coffee bean roasters and a prince of the county. Certainly there were some sticky issues and a few relationships more confounding than others, but life and ministry is what is; there are always difficulties in the midst of blessings.

It was one of the joys of my life to be able to influence teens and young people. With Wesley and Jonathan providing catalytic energy, we launched a drama team called *The Six-Eight Players*. The world premiere was well-received, which meant that drama became an important ministry tool for the first few years. It also had significant impact in the lives of several of the original players.

Another area where seeds flourished had to do with adventure and global awareness. In our time at Morrison, short-term summer mission trips were essential aspects of vision. A total of twelve teens were motivated and mobilized to accept the challenge, and two adults on separate years volunteered to go as leaders. One particular teen was a repeat offender into her twenties, and after graduating college and doing a stint teaching high school, she's now in full-time service for a missionary organization. I continue to pray that all those seeds will, in God's timing, produce positive results.

A milestone was reached at Morrison. It was an occasion that I had knowingly accepted the challenge of way back in 1972, but had done my best to run away and hide from it. In doing so I ended up on a rocky trail loaded with pitfalls that messed me up and harmed those whom I loved the best.

For a long while I'd lost my way, but in his pursuit of me, God unleashed grace that tracked me down and wouldn't let me go. God outlasted my stubborn stupidity, which is a marvel to me and was worthy of a party in tribute to his faithfulness.

On a Sunday afternoon in March 1998 the congregation hosted the celebration for my ordination. It was a special event that saw family and friends travel from Canada and Iowa. Each of our four sons had a role in the service, which was fitting and proper. After all, they'd experienced the rollercoaster ride of my life. They'd suffered through my exile and eyewitnessed my desperate fight with the One who called me.

Their participation honored me in ways I couldn't express then, so I will now. They gave me hope that day; hope that the wounds I'd inflicted on them while in the belly of a beast could be healed by the same redemptive love that refused to give up on me. It's a hope that remains ingrained in me in the form of prayer.

Shortly after the affirmation of my call and gifting, my boundaries for ministry were greatly expanded as denominational assignments began coming my way. I never went looking for any of the jobs, but when tapped on the shoulder, I gave every task the best I had to offer, which always seemed to result in another new avenue of responsibility.

There were conference-sponsored workshops where I gravitated to like-minded colleagues; there were many opportunities for training and exposure to dynamic, cutting edge ideas, all of which gave me insights and inspiration to keep developing ministry skills.

My writing also rushed through several wide open doors. For so long I had clung to the creative part of me with a two-fisted fierceness, but it was now coming alive in ways that astounded and delighted me. It wasn't isolated, but had outlets that garnered feedback, which was rewarding and humbling.

There was a graveyard on the edge of town that was perfect for early morning walks, which allowed me to stay true to my exercise program while considering my mortality in the midst of granite markers. My strenuous walking may have kept my eyes fixed on eternity and been good for healthy heart and lungs, but it was having a detrimental effect on the left hip.

The limp was aggravated as the bothersome pain became unmanageable. On the advice of our family physician I began toying with different options available to remedy the pain. I had many major doubts. Given my addictive nature, I didn't want to take narcotics and figured I was far too young for any surgical procedure, but would soon discover that the damage was excessive.

In January 1999, thirty years after the original fracture, I had hip replacement surgery at CGH Medical Center in Sterling, IL. The orthopedic surgeon was a nice man named Shawn. He listened intently to my story, and we looked at the X-rays together. They revealed that the ball of the femur was flattened out on one side, and the joint had severely deteriorated. He wondered how I could even function, then filled in some particulars as to what he suspected had actually happened on that ballyard in a whole other country and in what seemed to be another lifetime.

In our exploratory discussions, he sounded like a carpenter more than a doctor as he explained the process. He also promised me two things. First, the operation would result in a meaningful reduction of pain and potentially could eliminate it. Second, he guaranteed that if I followed his instructions as to post-operative therapy and care, the implant would last at least ten years without any problems, and perhaps much longer. Both promises have proven to be true.

The early weeks and months of recovery were remarkable. There were daily surprises of increased mobility and flexibility. And the absence of pain amazed me.

There was one side effect to that which was humorous. I couldn't sleep the night through; I'd awaken at two or three in the morning and be wide alert. I fought it at first, then gave up because my mind was popping with ideas. I'd get up, go to another room, and make notes or watch television.

One night it occurred to me that the reason for my restlessness was that the portion of my brain that had for years been engaged in repressing the pain was unemployed, so it was active and ready to party. I don't know if that's a medically accurate explanation, but it made sense to me and caused a few smiles. Eventually normal sleep patterns returned.

Taking all the variables into consideration, ministry at Morrison was grand. It was an adventurous cell in the body of Christ that responded to some big pictures about growth and development. We took *Church*

On The Road and had lots of fun stirring embers in people's hearts into flames. Lives were transformed, perspectives were stretched, and in it all, a few hard lessons were learned.

Our goals outreached our grasp. We didn't quite get to where we agreed we wanted to go, and for that I shoulder my share of responsibility, but I don't bear the burden alone. People are people, and unfortunately, more often than we recognize it, the baggage we all lug around clashes in ways that are detrimental to the advancement of the Kingdom.

Playing second-guessing games are easy, but not helpful, so I refrain from engaging in them. It's enough for me that I journeyed with a family of disciples for over a decade, and mostly we respected each other. Mostly we endeavored to know Christ and worked together to reflect him to others and make a difference along the way. In a fallen world, sometimes that's the best that can be achieved.

One story about the Morrison congregation must be told because it illustrates well the depth of the relationship we enjoyed.

In June 2003, when Wesley was arrested, I was completely open with the congregation; in fact, perhaps too honest.

I was emotionally naked with them, which can be dangerous and ultimately proved to be a relational wedge for some individuals to wield. Of course, what can anyone say or do in such heart-wrenching circumstances?

The Leadership Team led by example, supporting us unconditionally. We were broken, and at times their empathy was palpable. I had a long established breakfast or lunch schedule with many of those in leadership roles. In the aftershocks of this gaping fissure in our lives, those meetings took on a subdued tone. I was ministered to more than I ministered.

One intuitive gentleman, who'd been walking the talk with me all along, was especially accommodating. For purposes of obscurity and anonymity, he'll be referred to as Metazeta, though I refuse to change faces or rearrange scenes. He kept pace and never wavered. He granted me the freedom to express what human apprehension and disillusionment looks like at the gut-level, with the rough edges intact. Throughout the doubt-filled months that followed, he'd slip me little pieces of wisdom from Scripture at always just the right time.

I'm convinced that the majority of the congregation rallied around us because of the Leadership Team's attitude. One member had an idea to surprise me with a special gift as a token of encouragement and appreciation. I'm not sure how she sold it to everyone or if it was a difficult sale to make, but am grateful she did so.

It was a present that'd change my life and required agreement and coordinating with Anita, which was all done without any news leaking out along the grapevine to me. I was kept entirely out of the loop, so when it was sprung, I was dumbfounded.

The last Wednesday evening of September was when everything was set to happen. It was our *Souper Club*, a mid-week meal together, which I noted was unusually well attended; the church basement was packed. It seemed like *everyone* was there, which should have been a tip-off for me, but I was just pleased to have a crowd gathered.

When it came time for me to share a short devotional and lead a prayer time, someone stopped me, pulled up a chair, and told me to sit down. I gave him a quizzical look, but he insisted on me taking the seat, so I did.

Everyone was staring at me with big eyes and even bigger smiles. A moment later, a lady named Dana entered carrying an extra-large gift bag that was all bright colors and ribbons. Her face was lit up as she said a few extremely kind words about how wonderful I was and how much the congregation cared for me, and then handed over the bag.

I set it on my lap, but it seemed to move by itself, so I shifted a leg to balance it. I peeked inside and began pulling out fluffy white tissue paper, when all of a sudden I froze up because a pair of eyes where looking at me out of the darkness of the bag. I reached down, felt the warmth of a tiny body, and lifted it.

Being speechless is a trait seldom seen in me, but a little fur-ball of a puppy made it so. My tongue-tied affliction lasted for a long while as I tried to focus my thoughts into words. She was a Shetland Sheepdog who'd been born on August 4th, which gave her the name Augustina, but she gave it back. For reasons having to do with lonesome badlands and bandit doves, she prefers to be simply known as Gus, thank you very much.

Children crowded around to pet her. I cradled her like a baby as tears filled my eyes which I wanted to rapidly blink away and hide. Sure, it was the tri-colored hairball tugging at my heartstrings, but more than that, it was the realization that I was being touched by a brush of agape-style love.

Gus has become a close friend and confidant. She has a gentle tenacity that somehow softens me. She understands every word I say and even obeys when she's in the mood to do so. Her instinct to herd has provided hours of laughter along with insights into spiritual truths about human nature. Many of the early morning hours spent writing this found her curled up under my desk, eyeing me from time to time with an expression that says: *Are we going for a walk or what?*

There's likely no way to measure how important this genuine act of love has been for me. In the context of sorting through the emotional fall-out resulting from Wesley's crime, it likely contributed to my spiritual well-being.

While the justice system slowly churned along at a maddening and confusing pace, my shaggy-coated companion has been a living embodiment of trust and innocence.

After that early morning shock of a phone call and initial visit in June 2003, as far as it's been possible for us to do so, we've walked with Wesley each step of the way. To say that Anita and I were devastated is akin to remarking that the oceans are full of water. The pain can still wash over us incessantly, but fortunately our love and faith sank deep roots that are intertwined with a complexity that allows us to sustain and support each other.

All the *what ifs* and *if onlys* faded into the noise, but still resurface on occasion at particularly low points. Each time they bubble up to the top and beckon our attention, the choice is always the same. We can wallow in the unknown misery or choose not to be influenced by them. God being our helper, we endeavor to stay on the later course of action.

For me, in the weeks, months, and perhaps even years following the crime and our knowledge of it, I moved through the tasks and assignments of my job encased in numbness. Shallow concerns of ministry were accentuated and began sticking in my craw more and more. The pettiness we humans are capable of granting importance made me smile sadly. None of the frivolous matters could be avoided, but instead of being issues requiring my intervention or prayers, they became the humor that kept my senses glued together.

Does it really matter if themes or info on the church bulletin board gets changed too slowly? Am I truly supposed to tell God that so-and-so requires the specific job for which he or she have applied? Exactly when did I acquire the omniscience to know God's perfect will? I vacillated between wanting to shake people out of lethargy and force them to appreciate their comfortable lives or rub their noses in the very real brokenness all around us.

The minutia and deadlines of ministry were all accomplished in workmanlike fashion, but my passion and perspective took on a new fervor that was subtle on the outside, but quite obvious internally.

Eternity was constantly on my mind. All its compelling and profound mysteries captured me. Its promise of peace stirred up strength and spurred me forward. If at all credible or conceivable, my time spent alone in the graveyard took on even more substance as hope defied circumstances. I took an almost perverse joy in the knowledge that when my earthen body returned to dust, none of the crappy heartaches of life would matter one iota. And with that thought securely in mind, I pressed on.

Clinging to faith in a supernatural God who was working all things together for my good and his purposes became a conscious thing. Doubts were ever-present, but somewhere along the way I had determined that faith had nothing to do with the absence of doubts. Faith meets reality in that sweet spot where we learn to coexist with all those questions that have no tangible or satisfactory human answer.

An unnamed man in Mark nine became a quiet hero for me. He had an encounter with Jesus that sometimes gets glossed over far too easily. His son was trapped inside an ongoing torment that threatened his existence. The father was desperate to find help. It's likely that he had tried everything and sought out every possible option. He pleaded with Jesus for pity and mercy, and plainly, Jesus saw and had empathy for that family's anguish, but not so fast.

Before healing the boy, Jesus did something that on a lonely morning riveted me. He challenged the father's faith and the man replied, "I do believe; help me overcome my unbelief." *I do believe; help me overcome my unbelief.*

As I suspect God's Word intends, that's both good territory to explore and a solid place to stand. It wove itself in to become integrated into all my prayers. I had to repeatedly reaffirm truths and principles that from an earthbound perspective are paradoxical. In this, Anita and I mirrored each other.

In the wake of the shockwaves, we discovered Celtic Daily Prayer. We started using it in our daily devotions together and found renewed vigor in being connected to the faith-experience of ancient saints. The readings, coupled with Scripture, have an uncanny way of speaking to the immediacy of the moment. It occurs so routinely that we've decided that there are no coincidences in the pages, and the pages are no coincidences at all. The affirmation of the timelessness of God's character lifted us onto a path on which we still tread, for there are always more treasures to be unearthed along with the accompanying inspiration to push us upward.

We frequently find ourselves examining who God is in the context of our lives, which is a healthy perspective that requires much energy to keep it in alignment. We attempt to do so by presenting straightforward queries. What about any tragedy changes God's character? Does the all-knowing One take days off or go on vacation when troubles happen on planet earth? Omnipresence means being present in all places at the same time, so is it possible for God to forfeit that attribute?

Can God be rendered ineffective by any circumstance within creation? Did Wesley's rebellion take God by surprise, transforming him into a rinky-dink deity? Was God caught off-guard by the slow moving proceedings of the court? Did the crime and its consequences, as horrible as they are for everyone involved, rob God of his faithfulness? Was God somehow no longer sovereign?

The answer to all these questions and so many more that lurk around the edges of the human dilemma is the same: No. He is God; he's immutable, which means that he does not change, ever. Our hope is dependent on nothing less than the immutable character of our Creator. That knowledge must have an impact on hearts and perspectives or else it's all just a bunch of useless information taking up precious brain gigabytes.

It's not easy to regularly apply and put into action, but I'm persuaded that when we effectively implement an honest effort, the gaps of our failings are filled in with grace. When the father's faith was challenged by Jesus, he said, "I do believe; help me overcome my unbelief."

It was then and only then that Jesus responded by healing his son. One of the inferences in this passage that draws me in to hold me close is that our eternal and infinite God always makes allowances for our temporal and finite condition. While we're confined within flesh and blood, we require all the mercy God willingly pours out afresh each morning.

After more court dates and appearances than I can recall, it came down to Wesley's sentencing on a mid-September day in 2006. He'd been in the DeKalb County Jail for more than three years. There'd been numerous continuances and delays for reasons ranging from reasonable to outlandish. It was all difficult to follow. The criminal justice system is confusing and intimidating, and though I fully comprehend the English language, the dialect of legalese spoken in courtrooms has little or no relationship to English.

A phrase in a statute can be clearly defined and agreed upon, then moments later, when referenced by another lawyer, the exact same phrase can be framed to have an entirely different definition. Or an opposing statute will be cited that contradicts the previous statute, which, of course, rapidly solicits the citation from another case in support of the original argument. And back and forth it goes, professionals playing games of dueling nuance, with winners and losers determined almost arbitrarily.

Each court date and every conversation with lawyers resulted in unsettling bewilderment. We were swinging on a crazy pendulum, hanging on words that offered a tidbit of hope only to have that snatched away an instant later.

During the lengthy time in county lock-up, Wesley went through all the stages of grief. He underwent changes and transitions. A visceral sorrow mixed in with fear to keep him on edge. At the beginning, and I'm sure many more times than he let on, he was scared senseless. There was before and after the crime; his life and dreams had been totally altered.

No one could stand inside his shoes and see it through his eyes. No one could pay the consequences which would be required of him. Desperation cloaked him as he fought to find fairness balanced within justice, using whatever tools available to him in the system. He studied law books and got himself a jailhouse education.

More importantly, since *to know and serve God is all that matters in life*, he emptied himself and had a stunning spiritual experience. And when he did, God showed himself strong in his heart. His redemption story is reserved for him to relate in a venue of his choosing. It's sufficient to say here that it was real and radical. In the ensuing years, Wesley has demonstrated a wisdom and peace that can only be gleaned by cultivating a relationship with the One whose authority transcends earthly scales of justice.

It's necessary to note that the procedure which resulted in his sentence came about because of our son's prayerfully considered choice. There remained options available, but after so much time going up and down on the yo-yo of countless legal maneuvers, he willingly decided to accept whatever fate and future God had in store for him by throwing himself on the mercy of the court.

There had been a revolving door through which various lawyers entered and exited on all sides. Three different judges were involved, including a new one behind the bench at the sentencing hearing. The fact that a man from family court completely unfamiliar with the specifics could be assigned to pronounce judgment in a criminal case tells me that there's something drastically askew in the justice system. It disturbed me then, setting off alarm bells inside, and at some level it's still unnerving, but all such misgivings must be strapped onto the strength of God's sovereignty.

The promises of the presence of God found fulfillment in our lives on that day of judgment. If that were not so, we never could have overcome the heart-wrenching hours piled on top of each other. The courtroom drama was gripped by a tension that kept winding itself tighter and tighter.

The public defender serving as Wesley's attorney met briefly with us before the case was called to fill us in on what to expect and tell us the late-breaking news about the designation of the new judge. Though irregular, she was confident that the change would not be detrimental. She was a compassionate young woman who'd been handling the case for six months or so, and she'd shown herself to be knowledgeable.

At her counsel we had gathered two dozen affidavits from family and friends who had known Wesley before drug addiction had impaired his reasoning powers. She had submitted them all for the judge's consideration and was optimistic.

They brought Wesley into the courtroom with armed guards on either side of him. He was dressed in an orange jumpsuit with his arms shackled at his hips and chains around his ankles. The dehumanizing aspects of the system are sickening. He moved with a mechanical stiffness and stood behind a table beside his attorney. At the other table the District Attorney and the Assistant DA prosecuting the case stood, chatting quietly. We, Anita and I, along with a few other family members, were no more than ten feet behind. The victim and his entourage were also in the gallery, clustered together in a section off to our right.

With all the officers of the court in place, the proceedings got started with a detailed recitation of the crime. Its stark ugliness was transparent. Testimony was given by us, each taking their turn on the stand. The Assistant DA may have been a nice man in other circumstances, but in his domain, his domineering style bordered on vindictiveness. It appeared as though it was all personal for him; winning was all that mattered.

The victim and his girlfriend each told their story, urging the judge to lock the man who'd ruined their lives away for a long, long time. Their sorrow never stopped, and I found myself praying for them as they spoke.

At one point, the opposing lawyers dickered over a single phrase in a statute as though they were in a classroom in pursuit of academic goals. Tension must make time tick faster because hours disappeared in the testimony and questioning.

Finally, it was Wesley's turn to read a statement. It had been heavy on his mind. He'd prayed much on what should be included; the whole matter had been given a considerable amount of energy. As he began reading, his voice was strong, his bearing straight, his words clear.

Despite being chained he managed to maintain some semblance of dignity. His remorse was endless. The awareness of what he had done and the consequences for the innocent victim afflicted him deeply. He was guilty, and he took full responsibility for his actions. There was no casting of blame or making excuses. There were no mitigating circumstances. He'd made bad choices of his own free will. The addiction and what the drugs had done to him was his fault. He spoke of his upbringing and gave testimony to the rebirth of his faith in Jesus Christ.

With great sincerity and purpose, he apologized directly to the man he'd repeatedly stabbed, his voice breaking. He asked for the man's forgiveness, saying he fully understood if that were not possible. He swallowed hard, then thanked the court, and with that it was finished. If pride is the proper word or feeling in such a situation, then pride rose up in me. I was proud of my son.

The judge proclaimed a recess to consider it all. In a blink of time, perhaps twenty minutes, court was called back into session. The judge referred to his deliberations, saying that he had reviewed all the material facts, then in a cold, matter-of-fact manner pronounced judgment. There were two separate charges; on one Wesley received ten years and on the other nine years. Now the previous debate between the lawyers was no longer abstract or academic. It was over whether or not a particular phrase in a statue that applied here allowed the sentences to be served concurrently or consecutively.

There was more discussion. Concurrently meant he'd serve ten years; consecutively would require payment of nineteen years. I listened as intently as possible, and in my feeble understanding of legalese, it was evident that the wording was ambiguous enough to allow a judge certain leeway. If he was inclined toward mercy it'd be concurrently. If, however, he chose to enforce the letter of the law, he'd apply the term consecutively.

After consulting the Assistant DA about it in open court, which struck me as extremely out of order, the judge made his ruling. He chose to interpret the statute to mean consecutively. Wesley would get credit for time served, but the bottom line was that he was sentenced to nineteen years in the Illinois Department of Corrections.

The gasp that went through our family was audible, matched by the sigh of relief from the victim and the folks assembled around him. There was some shuffling of papers between the lawyers' tables, then it was all over. People moved around, and the courtroom began to clear.

The Public Defender had tears in her eyes as she told us how sorry she was that it'd turned out this way. She'd advocated with passion and determination, making arguments that on any given day before another judge would have received a different outcome; concurrent instead of consecutive. Our nerves were stripped raw. Her expression of empathy was comforting. I held her hand for a moment and thanked her.

A big, broad-shouldered bailiff left his post and walked straight to our son. He'd been present at nearly every one of Wesley's court appearances, and I'd often thought I should say a word to him, but had never followed through and actually done so. He moved with a military posture, and I thought he was going to simply pick up paperwork off the tables or escort Wesley out of the room, but instead, as our son began to stand, the man took an elbow and pulled him close. He whispered something in his ear, looked Wesley full in the face, nodded and left the room.

Wesley tilted his head and watched him disappear behind a door, then turned in our direction, his face contorted into a mask of awe and fear. His mouth was hanging open in a huge circle, his teary eyes wide.

Later that evening, we were allowed to visit him before he'd be shipped out to Statesville Penitentiary the next day to be processed. Wesley's voice was calm, his demeanor assured when he filled us in about the incident with the bailiff. When the broad-shouldered man pulled him in tight he said, "Son, I do not care what you did. You're a brother in Christ. Don't worry. God will take care of you." Peace radiated from our son's eyes, which amazed us.

In being obedient to an inner prompting, that civil servant modeled Christ-like love by delivering a message of inspiration. In a moment of sheer agony, he demonstrated the presence of God. It was almost an angelic visitation. It made me goosepimply; it gave me hope.

God will take care of you. It became my never-ending prayer for our son. The kind and considerate action of the bailiff furthered my comprehension that, in all the heartbreaking distress of life, I wasn't alone; we were not alone.

6

Epilogue

"The heart of the wise is in the house of mourning, but the heart of fools is in the house of pleasure."

~Solomon~

O N A FEBRUARY MORNING in 2009, we were thwarted in our plan to visit Wesley. We'd gotten up in the middle of the night to drive five hours to southern Illinois so that we could spend four or possibly five hours with him, and then return home.

We've attempted to make the trip every six weeks or so, wanting to do whatever we can to support and help him stay connected to the outside world. We arrived at a few minutes after nine, which is the regularly scheduled time visitation is supposed to begin. The facility is low and ugly, surrounded by a tall stainless steel fence crowned by large coils of razor-wire. It's a foreboding place that never fails to set off a slow burning nervousness that settles in the pit of my stomach.

On this particular day, we were greeted by a sign on the door of Lawrence Correctional Center that read: *Level One Lockdown. No Visitors Allowed.* We looked at each other, wordlessly communicating our immense powerlessness.

It took a moment to discover that the door was unlocked, and when we did, we tentatively entered the waiting area. We talked to the guard behind the glass, and though he appeared sympathetic, we were bluntly informed that there were no exceptions. *No Visitors Allowed* meant exactly what it said.

The lockdown began late the previous afternoon, and he told us that there was no way to know how long it would last. We offered an urgent protest, explaining the distance we'd driven, but he simply kept shaking his head. There was no appeal. They accepted a magazine we'd brought for Wesley, but that was all. We had to turn around and drive home without even being allowed to write a note and have it delivered to our son.

Frustrated, with discouragement and helplessness raking us, we returned to the car and left the parking lot. I'd like to tell you that I burst into a jubilant song of thanksgiving. I'd like to tell you that peace swelled up within me and found expression in praise. I'd like to tell you all of that and more fine things that'd reflect well on the vast depths of my faith, but if I were to do so, I'd be a boldfaced liar.

My initial headstrong reaction wasn't gratitude to God for his many blessings or even resigned acceptance of the situation because wretchedness remains rooted in me. I was angry. My teeth were clenched so tight my jaw hurt, when all of a sudden, less than a quarter mile from the prison, a big Red-tailed Hawk flew directly across our path.

It had jumped off a telephone pole and swooped across the road twenty yards in front of us. Before I even consciously thought it, the sight automatically triggered a silent prayer: *Thank you, Lord, for your kind protection on my life.*

A chill tingled through me. Then there was this heart-strong response which began to dismantle the primal headstrong one. I was still upset, but being in that mode doesn't change the fact of God's presence. I asked Anita to pray for Wesley's safety. She did, and then, as I delivered an eloquent soliloquy about the heartless unfairness of it all, I relaxed inside a calm assertion that everything was as it should be. This happened for a reason, and God was in control. The disruption of our plans wasn't anything that had meaning beyond his purposes.

As the miles were gobbled up, not for the first or prayerfully last time, we were astonished by the number of Red-tailed Hawks we saw on the way home. Obviously God knows when we need a special outpouring of encouragement.

~ ~ ~

Here are some conclusions drawn from an ordinary story: Life is preparation for eternity. It is an arduous refining process fired by hardships and difficulties. We can wish it were not so, but outside of fantasyland, those wishes will be unfulfilled. We can even stomp our feet, hold our breath, and throw a temper tantrum over it, but reality will remain unchanged.

For short spans of time we can use the wealth of affluent North America to insulate and isolate us from adversity and suffering, but much sooner than one realizes, the relentless and wearisome severity of the human condition will triumph. No amount of money will ever purchase an exemption from the uncertainty and natural vicissitudes of life.

Sorrow has many faces, all of which are equally difficult to look upon. Going eyeball-to-eyeball with it is never a pretty experience. Those struggles cannot be escaped because loss is commonplace. People think grief has to do only with the death of a loved one, but in the sin-racked world in which we live grief permeates all avenues of life.

However, grief isn't the enemy; the brokenness that comes with it isn't the enemy. We'll always hurt over something. We'll always miss someone. Grief is a force that shapes our character and perspective whether we recognize it as it is happening or not. Our response to it is crucial.

Some say that we're to simply get over sorrow and get on with the rest of our lives. The implication is that grief or loss is a fence we climb over and put forever behind us. Not so, for there are lessons to be learned while immersed in mourning which grant us wisdom.

We must travel through sorrow, and there are no shortcuts. We must burn the bridge of denial immediately so that we can join hands and walk along with bereavement, confronting all its accompanying doubts and questions in honesty. One cannot circle a date on the calendar with an expectation that when that day arrives, the distress of his or her remorse will be over.

Sorrow lasts a long time; a lifetime, in fact. There are particularly hard seasons when heartaches stack up upon each other to form a weight that threatens to crush us. Sometimes grief accumulates to the point of madness, and in those dreadful moments, it's only God's grace that can keep us putting one foot in front of the other.

Certainly there are incredible joys along the way, and we ought to celebrate and treasure every one, for the good times become the ballast that keeps us upright. There's wonder each morning; each day should be enjoyed as a miracle for the plain reason that the gift of the next sunrise isn't promised to anyone. Our days pass with bits of beauty seared by troubles, and no one can figure out what seemingly random events will be used to fashion us into the person God created us to be.

We so easily forget that we're works in progress. We so easily forget that God is actively working all things together for our good and his purpose. We so easily forget that all our ways are known to our Maker and he is not in the condemnation business. We may engage in bouts of self-flagellation, but God won't beat us down. He makes allowances for our humanity with grace and forgiveness which, when applied, lifts us up ever closer to him.

Grace is in symbiotic partnership with forgiveness. Grace empowers us to receive forgiveness, then we're to live in a state of forgiveness. We're to forgive those who wrong us and even those we *perceive* have harmed us. God wronged me, or at least that was the perception that deceived me. For many lost years I blamed God for accidents that scarred my adolescence and lashed out at him with a furious determination that fed on itself. Had I responded differently, perhaps my future wouldn't have been swallowed by a beast that had no mercy, though there's no way to know because *ifs* and *buts* have no true meaning.

What is reliably trustworthy is the hope that resides in forgiveness. For me to be bathed in hope meant that I had to forgive God, which by manufacturer's design required me to actually accept his everlasting offer of forgiveness and also to forgive myself.

It's strange how forgiveness works. When the forgiveness factor is activated, it has a repetitive program written into it which gives it self-perpetuating qualities. Forgiveness is an extravagance that we're to disperse and give away with the same measure we receive it. Our ability to shed the sludge this world dumps on us is tethered to our willingness to receive and give forgiveness.

Five hundred years before Socrates, Solomon of Israel penned a mind-altering treatise which explored the full spectrum of life on planet earth. It strips away all pretense and prettiness to delve into the marvelous and the mundane. We know it as Ecclesiastes.

I first discovered it as a teen-ager, and it has intrigued me always. From beginning to end, it's a superb piece of wisdom literature that demands much more respect than it usually receives in contemporary circles. Some complain that its tone is far too pessimistic for modern life, but those who reject it are destined to miss its comprehensive message of hope. Its dire warnings and stern observations are to be internalized. It's stark realism delivered by a man who had experienced all the pleasures that come with wealth and power only to determine that every bit of it was hollow and fleeting. None of what he reached for could satisfy for long, and ultimately there was no meaning to be obtained in any of it.

When examined in the full glare of reality, Solomon confirmed that life was hard, and the only thing that mattered or provided meaning was our spiritual journey and our relationship with the eternal and supernatural Creator. Everything else comes to nothing.

In exile, when my life was ebbing its way toward a reeking trash heap, I picked through bits of pain and fragility in search for significance. I came at it in a wildly irrational manner, blanketed in remorse and shaking a fist at God, but beneath that bitter and vulgar veneer beat a heart desperate for peace. I scraped and clawed at it as a starving man would reach for a crust of bread.

Late one night, I was alone in my basement bunker of an office drifting along in the emotional wake of Grandma Major's funeral. Some old familiar sad songs were playing on the stereo, with the volume turned low because the house was quiet. Everyone else was sound asleep. I was weary, but sleep refused my need, so I was deep into an excavation of Scripture that in those moments clutched hold of me. Three verses from the seventh chapter of Ecclesiastes grabbed me by the vitals.

"It is better to go to a house of mourning than to go to a house of feasting, for death is the destiny of every man; the living should take this to heart. Sorrow is better than laughter, because a sad face is good for the heart. The heart of the wise is in the house of mourning, but the heart of fools is in the house of pleasure."

I read them again and again. I closed my eyes to consider them or maybe even pray them, though I'd likely not acknowledge that then. Dylan was coming over the speakers singing a song about the night playing tricks and people being stranded while doing their best to deny it, and his lyrics mingled with Solomon's words, which set off what had to be a panic attack.

My throat cramped as though fingers were squeezing it. The discomfort spread down to become a spasm of tightness across my chest. I hitched in a whole bunch of little breaths, then exhaled them in a gust that released the contractions as suddenly as they had appeared.

The symptoms were most certainly the result of my mood and exhaustion, but they jolted my attention. I was fixated on those three verses. I read them in context of the whole chapter, then came back to them, turning their meaning over in my mind like a gardener using a spade to mulch dirt.

The idea that my perception was skewed by the night worried me, but soon that was gone, leaving me with nothing but the words leaping off the page like living things. I mulled them over, examining them from every angle I could imagine. They were upside-down principles. *Sorrow is better than laughter; the heart of the wise is in the house of mourning.* The problem of them kept returning, and it was long past dawn before it'd been worked out to a tenuous resolution.

I was nowhere near wise enough to identify it then, but what had happened was that while being consumed by galling animosity directed at God, I'd unconsciously applied the truth of this passage by submerging myself in sorrow. When comprehension penetrated the darkness these upside-down principles became the framework through which I filter all the vagaries of life.

Given that, it's no surprise that Jesus promised that those who mourn would be comforted. Jesus was fully acquainted with sorrow; the prophet Isaiah referred to him as a man of sorrows. It's my considered idea that the first human feeling Jesus had to deal with was sorrow.

When Mary delivered him in that cattle stall, and he drew his first breath imprisoned in human flesh, the shock of it all had to have found expression in a burst of wailing unmatched before or since. He'd been present at creation in communion with the Father. He was equal to the Father, yet he set aside his Divinity and stepped out of eternity in obedience to the Father's plan and purpose.

It had to be extremely traumatic for the babe swaddled in that manger. The substance of heaven's glory contrasted with the dilemma of the human condition. I imagine that it was a clash that jarred him pitilessly. The reality of flesh and blood, with its confining limitations and ever-present brokenness, must have caused huge waves of sorrow to wash over him.

When I read his promise of comfort for those who mourn, I take into account his initiating experience at Bethlehem. I also understand that he had full knowledge of the cruel injustices he'd be subjected to on a journey to a place called Golgotha, where heavy hammers were used to nail him to a Roman instrument of torture. His humiliation was immeasurably frightful, hanging naked in a public thoroughfare as he slowly suffocated and bled to death. Man of sorrows, indeed.

Yet in his most famously quoted sermon, he proclaimed, "Blessed are those who mourn for they will be comforted." On its surface that's sweet empathy, but it's not that simple. Those words carry a deafening gravitas that is enlightenment personified.

Life is process. Twenty years after that midnight discovery in Ecclesiastes, I'd get a glimpse of the brightness of God's Word gleaming directly on the tangled mess my life had been. On one of my graveyard walks, with Gus running circles around the stones, a flash burst into my mind so glaring that I stopped in my tracks. I'm not sure how long I stood still ruminating on the idea, but I do know that it was long enough for my shaggy-coated friend to become impatient.

Gus came close and barked several times to let me know she had places to go. I hushed her and started moving as my brain was busy unpacking a mesmerizing connection. Solomon wrote about the wisdom of hanging out in the house of mourning; Jesus promised comfort for mourners. It seemed so obvious, yet it had never crossed my path until that day.

The depths of it are still being probed, but the gist that keeps coming back is this: We mourn and comfort is available. It's circular, and in the comfort there's wisdom about mortality and our final destiny. Sorrow surrounds us and then, if we're open and willing to receive it, we're blessed by comfort that produces wisdom to live meaningfully. We mourn, we are comforted and in the transaction, by osmosis, we learn to value the things that are truly precious.

Life rushes in with abundance, for we come to fully realize that it can be radically altered or gone in a wink of time. Relationships become worthy of the continuous application of the forgiveness factor. The more we mourn, the more we're comforted, the more we discern what's important in the grand scheme of eternity.

The heart of the wise is in the house of mourning; blessed are those who mourn for they will be comforted. Linking those together philosophically may be enough to generate interesting musings, but putting them into practice will be transformational.

Sorrows of all kinds are inevitable. Train wrecks occur in our lives or in the lives of our loved ones. Circumstances come into play over which we have no control whatsoever. We get pinched in financial pliers.

We get trashed because of decisions made by others. A church dies and is buried. A ministry withers on the vine. Irreparable mistakes are made. We live with grievous consequences year after year.

Sorrows are everywhere, with the death of loved ones, natural or otherwise, being the place of ultimate mourning. Yet in God's provision, we have the tools to live in an endless cycle of mourning and comfort which is enriching in that it helps us remain focused on the eternal. The question is whether we choose to employ Kingdom values or merely capitulate to the cultural norms.

Emotions can be difficult to master and often betray us. We desire to live out the ideals that command our mindset to stay fixed on heavenly matters, but routinely fall short and muck along in mediocrity. We're shackled to the dictates of our wiring and makeup much more than we realize. We each have weaknesses that have been personalized just for us. The refining fires burn and extract impurities, which, with grace, allows incremental improvements or strengths to be revealed here or there, but it's slow going and always requires exerting lots of spiritual sweat.

When we struggle or fail to live up to the high standards of Scripture, defeat always beckons, but instead of giving in to it, we should take hold of the fact that God appreciates our unique design, and our feelings are no mystery to him. He's knowledgeable about grief and the sense of abandonment that tags along with it. He knows helplessness is real, with its handmaidens of fear and anger. When we knee-jerk react to these all too human feelings in a negative manner, the sincerity of our faith-walk isn't diminished and neither does God heap judgment on us.

It's mystifying, but God is our biggest fan, and his active purpose in our lives is to get our perspective pointed in the right direction, which is always an ongoing exercise. Our vision needs to be regularly adjusted and fine-tuned on the universal truth that our physical lives are temporary.

Life is short, and eternity is long; not at all an original concept, but one we must relearn by constant repetition. We claim to comprehend the brevity of life, but frequently our attitudes live outside the influence of the purported knowledge. The essence of all that mortality teaches us leaks out of our brain with a stunning ease.

What causes awareness acquired in the house of mourning to disappear so rapidly? Is it fear, the pain of loss, or just the running to and fro of life? Likely some of each, though my suspicion is that fear is the

primary culprit. Fearing the great unknown of death can be immobilizing, but it doesn't have to be that way.

For believers in Jesus Christ the masterpiece of our lives remains
unfinished until death has its way with us. For believers in Jesus Christ,
death is simply a passageway to another dimension. We know this to be
true because Jesus told us so.

It was in the Upper Room shortly before he'd be framed by religious
bigots who'd manipulate the system in the name of their religion. He was
teaching about eternity. He said that we ought not to be worried or concerned or afraid, using the metaphor of a mansion to describe heaven.
It remains a fascinating word picture. He was going on ahead to prepare
a place for us, and one day we'll join him. Death is just going through a
door into a room especially arranged for us by our Lord and Savior.

Along with the other apostles, Paul of Tarsus grasped this truth. He
lashed it around his heart and mind with vigor and fierceness. Fueled by
the power of its freedom, he fearlessly confronted potentates and princi-
palities. He was a step and a half away from dying in numerous ordeals.
He was beaten, whipped, stoned, shipwrecked, and in danger from all
sides. He suffered hunger, thirst, and nakedness. Time and again death
had him in its crosshairs, yet he pressed on in his passionate pursuit of a
more full relational experience with God.

When he was an old man, cooped up in a Roman jail because of his
uncompromising proclamation of the death and resurrection of Jesus
Christ, he wrote to his friends at Philippi. In one section of the letter,
he boldly told them he was in extreme conflict over life and death. He
resolved the quandary by saying that, if it was up to him, he was eager
to go through that door, but it was better for them that he stay put for
awhile longer.

There are days my heart rejoices in much the same manner.

One evening a couple days after the *Level One Lockdown* incident, the
phone rang. The display indicated that it was the billing service that
facilitates calls from the Illinois DOC. Anita answered it, listened to
the recorded instructions, then pushed the necessary button to be connected to our son. She chatted with him for a few seconds, then handed
the phone to me.

"Hey, son. You okay?"

"I'm fine, Dad," he said, sounding cheerful.

"What happened?"

He chuckled in a familiar way. "You know they aren't real forthcoming with news around here. What we were told was that there was a big fight in one of the cell blocks, so the whole place got locked down. It lasted until yesterday."

"We tried to get in, but no chance."

"Yeah. I got that magazine you left, so I knew you'd been here."

"They wouldn't even let me jot a note on one of the pages."

"As you know, the masters make the rules," he replied, referencing a song lyric I often quote. In my mind I could see his smile. We talked of life for awhile, hashing over serious matters along with some inconsequential fluff. Each call has a strict time limit, so we keep an eye on the clock and tend to share the valued minutes. When my time was up, I passed the receiver back to Anita.

It's always good to hear his voice. Given the unyielding situation, Wesley is doing well. His spirits are generally upbeat and positive. No doubt he has some bad days when the surroundings and circumstances gnaw at him, but mostly he has a constructive outlook. He strives to maintain it by nurturing his spiritual journey and keeping his perspective centered on the big picture. With the future clearly in his mind, he's earned an associate's degree and is continuing classes toward his bachelor's degree.

Correspondence is an essential lifeline to the outside world. God uses the infusions of encouragement to produce endurance that compels him to keep shining in the darkness. Wesley has developed a long list of pen pals and is regularly in contact with many of them. His rule is that, if he receives a letter from someone, he always replies. Anita and I are so appreciative and grateful for those who have been faithful in building a relationship with him. Only eternity will reveal the importance of these efforts.

The case is in the excruciatingly slow appeal stage. It started shortly after his sentencing, but then, for reasons that have never been fully explained, the appeal got shuffled away from anyone's attention. After dozens of phone calls, we've been assured that it's back on track, but who really knows?

From a layman's view, there are seemingly arbitrary gears within the system that easily malfunction. The bureaucracy—entirely disconnected from the lives involved—has its own policies and expectations that must be followed, and one soon discovers that fairness or common sense is seldom required.

The years pass while the legal procedure grinds along. There's no way to know whether something or nothing will result. Perhaps a different judge on another day will rule concurrent instead of consecutive. Or perhaps the proceedings and paperwork will once again become invisible or get misplaced in the labyrinthine halls of justice.

Only God knows, and unmistakably, in his faith-development plan for our family, we're to steadily trust him with the details. Whenever Wesley is released, we intend on having a blowout party because a son who was lost is now found.

We stand strong on Romans 8:28: "And we know that in all things God works for the good of those who love him, who have been called according to his purpose."

It's a promise that imbues our prayers with pragmatic solidarity. That, along with recognition and acceptance of God's will, entrenches us in the reality of faith. When Romans 8:28 is fastened to God's will in our lives, there's nowhere else to go except the reality of faith. There's no foreshadowing as to what winding turns lie in the road ahead, but in grace, we'll endeavor to persevere with every zig or zag.

For the last couple years we've been on an adventure in southern Ohio. The first decade of the 21st century has become history, which is an acceptable place to aim for some closure to this story.

Life continues, with struggles and joys. Its suffering and disappointments get bundled together with gladness and bliss, making life wondrous. I wouldn't trade my experiences with anyone. I wouldn't want to crawl inside anyone's skin because it's taken me half a century to figure out how to walk inside mine.

Our beautiful granddaughters now have two cousins, Christopher Alexander and Jacob Aaron, who are rambunctious and full of grit. Somehow each grandchild still thinks their grandfather walks on water, which is as sweet as life gets.

Also, as I write this, there is a sonogram on my computer of another grandchild , which cranks up anticipation. Boy or girl, it is still too early to tell. What we do know is that the baby is a tiny miracle of infinite wonder too marvelous for words; a reminder of the cycle of life and the mystery of faith.

I'd like to hang around this broken world long enough for the tall-tales at the family festivity for Wesley's homecoming, and also to dance at our grandchildren's weddings, but never presume to receive those gifts.

Perhaps every day is a good day to die. When the news gets out that they've stuck me in a hole or burned me in a kiln, please don't shed any tears for me because I'll be in the presence of Glory. Celebrate the fact that an ordinary life was blessed by extraordinary hope.

www.ingramcontent.com/pod-product-compliance
Lightning Source LLC
Chambersburg PA
CBHW051142020726
47501CB00005B/1627